The Texas Detective

A novel by Skoot Larson

Skoot's
Jazz
Books

ISBN: 10:0692513906

Published by Skoot's Jazz Books

Rockport, Texas

Dedicated to my old friend Dave Holman, may he rest in peace… Yes, Devorah, there really was a Dave Holman. He grew up in northern Minnesota, had been a railroad man and a private detective. When I met him, we both worked for a newspaper in St Petersburg, Florida. Dave and I were drinking buddies. He turned me on to the Holman martini, lots of gin with no real martini in the mix. Long after I left Florida, he would call me when the bars closed in that state to talk. I don't think he was ever in Texas, but the stories he shared with me prompted me to write this novel. Thanks, Dave!

Also, a special thanks to my editor, Theresa Feeser. Her dedication and attention to detail made this tale much more readable.

Rockport, Texas, is a real place and where I currently call home. Many of the geographic locations in this story are also real, but beyond that this is a total work of fiction. All the characters in this tale exist only in my twisted imagination and any resemblance between them and any person living or dead is purely coincidental.

PROLOGUE

It was a hot, sweaty afternoon in Rockport, the city that never wakes up, especially on hot sweaty afternoons. I was sharing an intimate conversation with the office bottle. I'd tossed a few wilted leaves of mint into the clear glass flask of scotch, so I could call it a mint julep. Mint julep was supposed to be good for hot, sweaty afternoons but gin usually worked just as well.

My office was above a local feed and fence store on a farm-to-market road leaving town. The rent was cheap. And even cheaper as I shared it with the local elephant rescue. There weren't many elephants to rescue in these parts, but it gave Yolanda a purpose. Yolanda had come to Rockport to waitress in an Indian restaurant, the India Palace, but the restaurant only lasted about six months, so she filed for non-profit status on her life, founded her rescue operation and started camping out in my office. She hung her little grey pachyderm shaped sign right under my shingle, Dave Holman, Private Eye.

She was a Pisces and drank like a fish, but she was good company when she was half in the bag. Even better when she was half out of it! At the moment, she was out on her bicycle looking for elephants to rescue. Most likely pink ones if she'd found her way to the Rusty's Tropical Café and Bar. At least the bicycling kept her in shape.

I heard the heavy footfalls of expensive high-heeled cowboy boots on the stairs even before I smelled the rank odor of stale cigar smoke. It was a short man in a tall brown Stetson and reflector sunglasses who entered my quarters and parked his frame on my plastic Walmart client chair. The man crossed his ankles, shot his cuffs and looked with disdain on my early Ikea furniture. His custom Western suit looked like it probably cost more than my first marriage!

"Can I help you, pal?" I asked him as I rested my supersized mint julep on the open lower lip of my desk drawer.

"Ah certainly hope so," the small man drawled. "Do you find missing things?"

"Depends on who lost'em and who's lookin'" I grinned back at him. "This lost thing you're lookin' for belong to you?"

"Ah certainly hope so," he repeated redundantly. "Ahm comin' up fa' reelection soon and I might sorely need it."

At first glance I hadn't recognized the Senator in his hat and shades. Television and newspapers usually portrayed him bare headed and sans reflectors. I wasn't sure what to say next. Yolanda was always accusing me of being politically incorrect, and she was right as usual. I hadn't backed a winner in a least a dozen state and local elections.

"I'm not getting involved in anything to do with campaign money," I stated bluntly. "If one of your people has their hand in the pot..."

"Not like that at all," he laughed hollowly. "I almost wish it was that simple!" His clock did serious again. "It's mah sense of humor, sir! Ah seem to have lost mah sense of humor!"

"So sorry," I gave him in deadpan. "But finding a conservative politician's sense of humor is about two light-years above my pay grade! Maybe you should try military intelligence?"

"That's very droll," he bristled sitting up straighter in his chair, "very droll indeed, sir! But this is a serious matter!"

"I'm sure it is," I replied, trying hard to suppress a giggle. "Maybe you sold it to one of your rich backers. If you remember which one, maybe you could ask for it back."

"If ah was lookin' for a smart mouth, I could'a called one of mah girlfriends, Holman! Now listen, I got plenty of money. Just name yo' price and let's get on with this!" He squirmed uncomfortably.

"Your first wrong assumption, Senator, is that I'd want to do anything to help you win another election!" I gave him my sweetest smile. "I kinda like what the other guy has to say about how he'd run the office. I think Texas has swallowed enough conservative tea-bagging. It's time for a change!"

"But that's just it, Holman! If I could find my sense of humor, I might just be able to see my way into some changes!" He started waving his hands around like an Italian used car salesman. "I can see the writing on the wall. People are gettin' tired of empty promises.

"If I could learn to laugh at myself, maybe I could laugh *with* them. I could be a true *good ol' boy* again! It'd be worth a shot."

"It might make you seem like a moderate," I warned him. "Maybe even, God forbid a liberal leaning moderate."

The man narrowed his eyes in my direction. "Son," he growled, "We are talking politics here. It's all about winnin'! If it takes lookin' like a commie-pinko-liberal to beat my opponent, so be it. I am in this race to win, God damn it!"

"Alright, Senator," I laid it on the line for him. What you've got to do is find your heart, your compassion. Find some love and respect for your fellow man!"

The Senator sputtered a few incoherent sentences, shook his head and then stared bug-eyed into my face. "You're serious, son?"

"Dead!" I answered.

"Well, if that's what it takes. Tan my hide and call me a southern Democrat! I *will* keep my seat in the government! Thank you Mr. Holman.

The Senator started to rise up from the green plastic lawn chair.

"Not so fast," I cautioned. "You owe me a check for five large!"

The man fell back into his cheap seat laughing uncontrollably. "I owe you?" He sputtered.

"Yeah, you're laughing, aren't you?" I gave a hearty guffaw of my own. "I'd say you've got your sense of humor back and then some. You told me if I could do that for you I could name my price!"

The Senator's hands shook as he wrote out the check. Yolanda would be happy tonight. When this buffoon's check cleared, I'd take her to Corpus for a vindaloo and a Kingfisher lager!

CHAPTER ONE

It was still hot and sweaty a month later, maybe even more so. I was out in that heat punishing myself with a walk on Rockport Beach. Even the water was hot, more like bath water than the normal gulf temperature. I was watching a pair of pelicans gliding over the small waves, doin' touch-and-go landings behind a small pod of porpoises while a scarlet phalanx of rosette spoonbills moved east to west overhead.

I was walking in ankle deep water along a shallow sandbar about fifty feet off the beach, treading carefully to avoid the occasional jellyfish that swam across my path. Wading along in the bay was my form of meditation, and I tried to take a walk here every day before I had my first drink. Yolanda said it was pointless to meditate after that first drink. I don't know if that's true or not, but it never hurt to humor her. I knew that after a few shots, my meditations could be more like nightmares, but that's another story.

I let my mind drift, becoming one with the surrounding water. I was almost in a true state of bliss when my cell phone started vibrating in the pocket of my gray cargo shorts. I thought about ignoring it. It would probably be just another text from the cell phone company reminding me how old my phone was and how I really should join the 21st century with a more up-to-date model, but I *liked* my old phone. I liked its two apps, talk and listen. They were all I needed. And sometimes, I thought, much more than I needed. What I really required was peace and quiet!

The vibrating continued, irritating me and screwing up my

calm, peaceful mental state. I answered it with a snarl to pass along that irritation.

"Holman, what the hell do you want?"

An infuriating chuckle filled my ear. "My, my, aren't we testy today, things not goin' good with the elephant girl?"

"What do you want, Senator? Lose your sense of humor again?"

"Sounds like you're the one a scoch short on humor today, Holman. I'm over at your office. I came by to see you, but you ain't here. Don't you keep some kinda normal business hours?"

"The business I do can't be done in an office," I told him. "I'm out in the field right now investigating!"

"You on some big case then? I got the impression your little detective agency wasn't really all that busy right now."

"Client confidentiality, I can't talk about what I'm working on!"

The little man's laugh was unnerving. Did he have people spying on me? And if he did, why was he waiting at my office? He could have just sent a carload of state cops or other thugs to pull me off the beach and drag me to his place.

"I don't need the smart mouth right now, Holman. Finish up your little beach walk. I'll be waitin' in my limo in front of your building. But do try to hurry up. Some of us think of our time as valuable."

I tried to think of a snappy come back, but the man had hung up.

I walked back to where I'd chained my bicycle, my usual walk only half completed, and peddled the shortest route back to my digs. Riding up Market Street, I could see the long white Lincoln poking just a few inches from the parking lot into the first lane of traffic. Getting closer, I could hear the engine ticking over and the labored breathing of the car's air conditioning. I could also see that Yolanda's elephant-gray 1960s Volkswagen Thing was in her reserved spot beside the outside stairs to the office along with her bicycle. Her bicycle was easy to recognize. It had pink rims, a pink seat and a gray pachyderm shaped placard bolted to the side of the old red milk crate balanced on her rear fender.

The Senator emerged from his chilly cavern as I was locking my bike to the side of the stairs next to Yolanda's. No big hat or boots today. The man was dressed in jeans, a ZZ Top tee shirt and a Spurs baseball cap, no shades. As he stood up from his white chariot and slammed the door, he motioned toward my office door with his head. When I hit the first step, the Senator was close on my heels. He closed the office door behind us when we'd entered and gave Yolanda an empty smile as he parked his bulky frame in my plastic client chair.

"Pardon me, miss, but I've got some sort of personal business to discuss with your b'wana here."

Yolanda gave him two eyes of steel. "I'm Holman's partner in this agency, and his back-up. I took the same oath of confidentiality. Just pretend I'm not here."

"Well, you see, ma'm. I'm kinda shy talkin' about confidential family shit in front of women, excuse my French. Nothin' personal, but could you grant me an indulgence here, just this once? If Mr.

Holman feels you need to know, he can tell you later when I've left."

Yolanda gave him a vacant look, but after a half a minute, she walked out and closed the door. Out the window, I could see her on her bicycle heading in the direction of town and the bars.

"Don't you dare repeat a word of what I'm about to tell you to that woman, Holman," he hissed *soto voce*. "It's embarrassing enough havin' to tell this to you!"

"So someone *does* have their hand in the campaign till, then?"

The Senator gave a hollow laugh. "I wish it was that easy! But it's my wife."

"Your wife is stealing from your campaign funds?"

"Hell no, Holman, it's, well, I, I don't want to be seen as less of a man..."

"I don't judge, Yolanda doesn't judge. We help people find lost things or people. We try to sort out people doing illegal things..."

"But you *are* a keyhole peeper too, right?"

"Not if I can help it. I don't like domestic work, especially divorces..." I let that hang in the air for a minute.

"Holman," the Senator barked, rising slightly from his chair. "My wife may be runnin' around on me. If my wife *is* runnin' around on me, that hurts my image as a strong, get-things-done kind of guy! Let me just be real frank with you, if my wife is cheatin' on me, seein' other men, it could cost me this election."

I sat still, giving him my finest blank expression. I had a strong urge to open the drawer and take a small slug from the office bottle. It was cheap Caribbean rum today, with a little coconut water added for some vitamins.

"And, like I've expressed to you before, I want to win." The volume of his voice was rising. "I always want to win! I don't care if I have to compromise some values, or sell out some of my backers, but I *will win* this election, even if I have to kill that woman!"

"I didn't hear that!" I probably said it too strong and forcefully. "Besides, I don't do divorce work if I can help it. Always ends up too messy, and half the time, I end up the big loser in the game. Spouses have a way of suddenly becoming all lovey and loyal again when it looks like they may lose money or security."

"Don't jerk me around, Holman! I'm a powerful man in this state! I can have your license! And that elephant girl's as well... if she's got one."

I remained stone-faced, but beneath the edge of the desk, my hands were shaking, jonesin' for a drink.

"I gave you a big lump of cash to establish what kind of man you were. I didn't mind, 'cause I found out you are an honest and dedicated fellow. You have a lot of traits I admire in a man. That's why I came here in the first place and that's why I'm here now!

"I also had my office do a bit of research. I know you were fired from the Los Angeles Police Department because you were a little *too* honest, and didn't like your fellow officers beatin' up blacks and homeless men without cause. I can't say if that's good or bad. Lots of black and homeless folks might just need a good ass kickin' now and then, but be that as it may, it demonstrates that you got ethics and a bit of character, things I'm in search of right now. When the L.A. Chief blocked you from getting a private ticket, you went home to Indiana and started an agency there, but you couldn't handle the cold weather after all those years in paradise, so you came down here. You'd been down here as a Coast Guard/DEA agent before you joined the L.A. cops."

"Yeah," I told him, keeping my poker face. "You got most of that right."

"And right now," he continued, "You don't got *nathen shaken*. You're close to maxed out on your credit and, in spite of the big check of mine you cashed last month, you're still way behind financially!"

His face lit up in an I-think-I-hold-all-the-cards grin. "So, can you do some checkin' for me on my wife? It won't be a divorce thing, I hope. That could be just as disastrous as folks knowin' she runs around. You just keep a close tail on that woman and report every little move she makes to me. If she is foolin' around, I'll send some of my boys to have a talk with her."

"Alright, Senator, but if she should turn up dead, all bets are off. Your confidentiality flies out the window and with it any chance of you ever even becoming the dogcatcher in a county with very few dogs!"

The man's empty smile said it all. He had me as he wrote out another large check. "Just in case you run up some expenses," he told me. When he left, I realized what my first expense would be. The level of rum and coconut water was dangerously low.

CHAPTER TWO

When the small man had left, I snapped right into action, going to the broom closet to check my supply of booze. It was low; too low to keep me going through a tough campaign. I decided I should go out to restock before I sat down to any serious detecting.

My old Saab fired up on the second try, and I took the highway out of town. I was headed for the Bottle Brothel, a small liquor store out in the sticks beyond the city limits. They did a thriving business among local fishermen and good ol' boys.

The old crusty bottle-blond who owned the place was always sitting in her rocking chair, puffing on a cigar on the store's shaded porch to vet the gentlemen who came to give her custom. Behind her heavily tinted windows, her three young clerks walked the four aisles of booze in corsets, dark stocking, white little girl socks and high heeled pumps. It was a great gimmick, especially here along the Bible belt, where folks took their sin seriously.

Yolanda was always pointing out that I could ride my bike to Spanky's Liquor, just down Market Street from the office. I'd be saving money on gas and the prices were lower. I'd also be supporting a local *Rockport* business and I wouldn't be promoting the exploitation of women.

I figured it was worth a little more for a bit of heart-quickening entertainment and besides, the Brothel girls were well paid exhibitionists. The old girl who owned the store probably paid them twice what they'd make at Spanky's and they didn't do anything but sell liquor. Any customer who tried to get fresh would find himself looking down the barrel of the owner's former husband's old army colt.

I loaded up my cart with a few bottles of Cluny Scotch, and a few more of Taaka Gin. I decided to pass on the rum. Then, thinking of Yolanda, I bought a case of a local Texas IPA, Redfish Ale, brewed in nearby Goliad.

"Just put it on my tab," I told the sweet redhead in the green and black brocade.

The girl snorted through a wicked grin and held her palm out. "Cash, Holman! Betsy says until you get your tab down under three figures, you don't have a tab. And even then, she said she'll have to think about it."

"You wound me, my dear! Betsy knows I'm good for it as soon as I cash the retainer check on my current case."

I heard the heavy steps behind me, then Betsy's rough smoker's voice close to my ear. "I'm very grateful to you for sorting out those two redneck boys who broke in last year and stole so much of my beer, but I have a business to run too. And the expenses that go with it... like paying these fine ladies who work for me. I want your bill paid in full within two weeks, or you won't be shopping here anymore. Is that clear, Holman?"

I turned and looked into her bright green eyes. "I'll be gettin' some money soon, Betsy. As a matter of fact, I just started a new case that I think is going to be worth some very solid bread..."

She just continued to glare at me as she accompanied me out of the store, reclaimed her rocker and fired up the stub of her stogie.

I opened the Saab and found my checkbook in the glove box, then ducked back out to face the old girl.

"So how much do I owe you? I can give you a check dated for next week, but it won't be good until then."

She blew a cloud of rancid smoke into my face. "Make it for two-hunnerd... No, wait, make it three hunnerd. *If* and when that check clears, I'll reopen your account and you'll have a little cushion on it."

Betsy took my check back inside and another of her girls, a twig thin brunette, pushed my cart of assorted bottles to the door. I loaded the booze under Betsy's watchful eye, then put myself in the driver's seat as she resumed her rocking on the porch in the ninety degree heat.

From the Brothel, I decided I had better make a bee line for my bank with the Senator's check. I needed it to clear before Betsy got the wild idea to test my check and before the Senator could change his mind!

Back at the office, I found Yolanda hunched over a laptop computer at her small desk in the corner. I set the cardboard wine box I was carrying on the floor and walked behind her to look over her shoulder.

"The Senator has a Master's in Humanities from UT Dallas in Plano." She told me without looking up.

"Why are you checking up on the Senator?"

"I was listening at the keyhole. I heard most of what he had to say and now I'm on the case."

"But I saw you ride off…"

"As far as the trailer park next door, then I doubled back and parked my bike on the other side of the building.

"Looks like the Senator used to be a dope smoking hippie as well! That's according to an old story someone's posted from the school's paper, but it doesn't say if he inhaled. Maybe he's worried that his wife is going to blackmail him."

"You know that eavesdropping isn't very nice!"

She popped the bubble gum she was chewing. "Hey, Dave, we're in a dirty business, okay? Do you know who old Cleghorn's brother-in-law is? None other than that irritating Corpus Christi preacher creep who's always shouting about the Bible and Christians being persecuted for their beliefs; the Right Reverend Clement Gordon!"

"Clem Gordon is the Senator's brother-in-law? You mean Senator Jenkins is married to Clem's sister?" The small screen my lady was staring at didn't make any sense to me, so I decided to sit down at my own desk.

"That's what I just told you."

"And where did you get Senator Cleghorn? That's an old radio character from Allen's Alley, a show that ended before you were even born."

"A former boyfriend had a collection of old radio shows on tape. I found them more interesting than *he* was." She blew another small pink bubble. "So are you interested in what I've found or not? It looks like Reverend Gordon's church is one of the top contributors to the Jenkins' political war chest at three-point-five million."

"Three-point-five million? Where did you get that?"

"The public has a right to know. Jenkins' office has to file reports with the state. It's all public record and available... if you know where to look. You really should learn to use a computer, Dave."

By now I was ensconced behind my desk. I opened the bottom drawer and brought out the nearly vacant rum bottle. I finished the tepid liquid in one swallow, coughed and thought for a minute.

"So our client probably owes a lot of favors to the Corpus Christi Church of the Eternally Blinding Light, like pushing an agenda of fundamentalist Christian ideals.... We really should be taxing those people!"

Yolanda gave a hollow laugh. "Yeah, I'd say your senator buddy has been bought and paid for by Clem Gordon's people. And with the debt he owes Gordon, I don't think he can say too much about how the man's sister acts. It looks like they've both got the man's nuts in a mangle!"

"A mangle?"

"A mangle, you know, like a ringer, is that what you call it? On old washing machines..."

"Okay, I got you." I got up and went to the box I'd set on the floor when I'd walked in. I dug around till I found one of the bottles of cheap blended scotch.

Yolanda took a quick glance over her shoulder and grinned. "You've been to that place with the girls in their underwear again? I hope you didn't soil your y-fronts on the way home."

"Come on, Yo, that's not fair. I just like to shop there. They're nice kids, and they let me run a tab…"

"Yeah, I meant to tell you. That Betsy woman called a few days ago to tell you she isn't giving you any more credit…. Hmm, this is interesting… before Gordon went off to divinity school, he was a classmate of Jenkins at the U.T. Doesn't say anything about Gordon being in with the hippies though."

I stood, cracked the bottle and went back to look over Yolanda's shoulder. When I'd taken a pull, she reached behind without turning her head, grabbed the bottle and brought it around to take a swallow herself. When she'd finished, Yolanda set the bottle on the edge of her desk then looked around, her eyes daring me to pick it up and have another drink too quickly. I picked it up and took another pull anyway.

"So," I mused. Jenkins and Gordon were at U.T. around the same time. We can't say if they were friends, or if they even knew each other. Was the sister there as well? What's her name, anyway?"

"She calls herself Bunny now. She's a few years younger than her brother. Real name is Elizabeth Anne Jenkins, nee Gordon. Unless she's posted her life story on Facebook, I don't know if the Internet could tell us if they knew each other way back then…. Good Christian girl, maybe the Senator knocked her up!"

"Yo, watch your mouth. The Senator is our client, after all, our *paying* client."

"So big deal, he's a man, isn't he? Got the same weaknesses as all you men, especially back then if he was young and into free love and dope!"

"Keep diggin', Yo," I told her as I leaned my head back and rolled the cool whiskey bottle back and forth on my forehead. "When you're done, maybe you could run a shadow on our Bunny and see what she's up to."

"Right on it, B'wana!" She turned and winked at me.

"Cut that B'wana shit," I told her. "We're equals in this. And I was gonna tell you about the case. You didn't need to be creeping around and listening at keyholes."

"Oh yeah, right! So let's go somewhere and celebrate that we've hooked a live one. Rusty's Tropical Café and Bar? You can spring for some fried crawfish tails and we'll talk it over."

CHAPTER THREE

"Bunny is married to Senator Jenkins?" Rusty asked. "I've never noticed her wearing a ring. She's been in here a few times, usually with some pretty high rollers. Most of them are pretty strange dudes."

"So you know the Senator's wife?"

"I know Bunny Jenkins, if that's the Senator's wife. She comes in here a couple times a week. Usually takes a table in the back corner by herself and entertains some characters who fall by, that Betsy woman with the whore house liquor store, for one. Bunny has dinner here, but her friends generally have a drink or two at her table, and seldom finish their drinks. They're in and out pretty fast."

"This doesn't seem suspicious to you?" Yolanda asked.

"Hey, guys, I run a restaurant and bar here. I don't follow my clientele that close as long as they pay their bill and don't cause a ruckus in here!"

"So, have you ever noticed anything out of the ordinary? Like money changing hands," I asked.

Rusty shrugged, but the day bartender, Cat, piped up. "I've been a bit suspicious a few times. There was a big pile of cash on the table one time. When they noticed that I had noticed, the folks covered it behind their hands and that lady, Bunny, quickly scooped the cash into her big straw purse."

"And you never said anything?"

"Hey, Dave. It isn't any of our business!" Rusty shouted.

Yolanda put a hand on Cat's wrist. "It's cool, Cat. Your job is to see to the customers here. There was no reason for you to be suspicious..."

"Well, I'm kinda curious now," Cat replied. "I'd like to know what's going on right under my own nose!"

"Don't sweat it, Cat," Rusty said. "It isn't our job to save the world."

"But you could be a big help," I told them. "If you can share information that might help us in solving this case..."

"And just what case is *this*?" Rusty wanted to know.

"I can't say too much."

"So back to square one," said the café owner in a mocking tone. "You want to clue us in to what's going on, maybe we can help. Otherwise..."

"Does this Bunny woman come here in a regular pattern?" Yolanda was riveting Cat with her serious dark eyes, "Certain days of the week, or times of day?"

"I think it's usually right after the lunch rush, when we're kinda slow between lunch and happy hour. And Mondays and Thursdays, I think."

"That's a big help," Yolanda patted Cat's wrist again. "Tomorrow's Thursday," she mused. "Dave, I think I need to come back here tomorrow for a late lunch..."

We ate our dinner, said goodbye to Cat and Rusty and headed back to the office. At my desk, I mixed Yolanda and me some martinis, long on gin, short on martini. Martini? I don't think we even had any in the office. The dusk was gathering. It gathered fast in our office as the windows mainly faced east. We sat in the quiet gloom for a long time. Finally, Yolanda broke the silence.

"One of us needs to start a tail on this woman. I could do it, if I can catch her at Rusty's tomorrow. She must follow some kind of pattern. Everybody does. I'll pick her up there and stay close on her butt, but not too close..."

"And that will tell us?"

"A lot! Does she have a number of boyfriends? Or lovers? Or other folks who put piles of cash on tables? Does she spend her days meeting strangers at places like Rusty's? And how close is she to her brother?"

"You've got a dirty mind, Yo."

She gave me a leer. "Isn't that why you love me?"

I started to protest, but she pulled up her blouse to reveal her bare brown breasts. "You're too easy, Dave!" she laughed. "So just admit it and follow me down the hall..."

CHAPTER FOUR

Yolanda left the office around one on Thursday afternoon driving her old Volkswagen Thing. It had to be early 60s, it didn't even have those larger tail lights the German car maker introduced around 1969. The car was light gray in color, with darker gray elephant logos on the doors that advertised her non-profit animal rescue service in day-glow orange. How can you run a surveillance in something so out-of-the-ordinary? Maybe there was some truth to the idea that the more outrageous you appeared, the more people tried to avoid noticing you.

I took a drive into Corpus Christi after she was gone. I cruised the south side of town, finding the Church of the Eternally Blinding Light in a lightly populated neighborhood off Hensohn Road, near the airport. It was a sprawling complex of modern brick and glass buildings surrounded by acres of parking lot and live oak trees. It brought to mind the Crystal Cathedral in Garden Grove, California, that had grown from an outdoor church started in the Orange Drive-in Theater back in the 60s. How had Clemson Gordon built such an amazing following in some forty years? It had to take millions every year in tithes to finance something like the complex I saw out the window of my old Saab.

I sat for a time, trying to count the many buildings and figure out what they might be. The three story glass A-frame in the center must be the main sanctuary. It looked to be nearly an acre in size. Through the clear sides, I could make out balconies at either end. If one was the choir loft, the other had to be some kind of second floor seating. Other buildings could be class rooms or other meeting rooms…

My thoughts were interrupted by a short blast on an electronic siren and flashing lights in my mirrors. A white urban assault vehicle with a logo of an eye superimposed over a scarlet cross on the open driver's door had pulled in close behind me. A dark-haired fireplug of a man in a white uniform, white Smokey-the-Bear hat and reflector sunglasses got out of the vehicle and walked up to my door. A sky-blue shoulder patch told me he was with God's Security.

"You got some business to be loitering around the church grounds," he asked with a chilly smile. "It's just that we've had some threats from some of these liberal Christian haters lately."

"Just admiring the place," I smiled back.

"Well, maybe you should be admiring it from a greater distance, like from the other side of the highway."

"I might want to join this church," I told him. "My life is kinda, you know, at loose ends right now."

"So can I see some ID, loose ends?"

"Have I done something wrong, sir?"

"Just break out that identification. We like to keep track of strangers who come by the church. If something should happen, like a bomb or a fire, we like to have a list of names to give to the police."

"Something should happen? Are you kidding? I said I was just curious!"

"Yeah, and fucking Arab pilots checking out the World Trade Center before 9-11 were just curious too. Now are you going to show me some ID or am I going to hold you for the city cops?"

I brought out an old fake California license I always carry introducing me as Eric B. Lindstrom. Reflectors carried it back to his truck and stayed there for a few minutes. Finally he brought my fake license back and told me, "You'll be leaving now. If we catch you hanging out here again, I'll be very suspicious... And you might find yourself coming to some physical harm!"

I caught the threat implied in his voice. "If I come back Sunday to attend a service here? Or to join the church?"

The man laughed at that, "Yeah, we'll see you Sunday. But even on Sunday, I'll be keepin' a close eye on you, so keep your nose clean, Lindstrom!"

When I got back to the office, after a couple fresh pale ales at the Seafood Station Restaurant and Brewery on the Corpus bay front, Yolanda was pulling a stack of paper from the office printer.

"My report, B'wana." She blew another pink gum bubble, popped it and gave me a big grin.

"Will you stop with that B'wana crap? What did you find? Anything interesting?"

"It's all in my report."

I went to the cupboard, grabbed a couple room temperature Redfish IPA bottles, opened them both and handed one to my Asian partner. "How about you give me a bit of verbal summary and I can file the report away for later?"

She took a long pull from her beer and thrust her chest forward at me. "Okay, Dave… Now that I have your attention, our Bunny led me on quite an interesting chase. From the bar, it looked like she bagged a few hundred bucks. The first pile from your Madam Betsy, then a bit more from a tattooed Latin kid with eyes that couldn't stand still and from a slick dude who could have been a politician, I don't follow things close enough to know who all the political guys are."

"Interesting…"

"I had some trouble picking up her trail from Rusty's. I couldn't exactly ride her tail pipe out of Fulton, but I guessed right that she's be headed for the 35, so I raced ahead to Market Street and waited by the onramp. Her Lexus flew by within three minutes and I was back on the case. She made a stop in Aransas Pass, another small storefront saloon. I waited across the street until she came out clutching her big straw purse, then she led me across the big bridge. She got off on Leopard Street, where a pair of sorry looking dudes were hanging out under the Crosstown Expressway in a little graffitied park. They exchanged cash for some small packages, dope came to my mind. These guys looked like meth freaks or worse. She hung there for a few more minutes and collected a bit more from a black dude dressed like either a soul singer or a top kick pimp, then it was off to church.

"Since my car's too obvious, I ditched it a block away and ran back to the church. I got a clear shot, thanks for the diversion by the way, 'cause the security guy was busy rousting you!"

"So you already know about my afternoon…"

She laughed. "Dave Holman, the master detective! Anyway, Bunny had parked in a special reserved space near that big glass building, then she'd crossed the lot to a smaller office building. She wasn't that conscientious about makin' sure the door locked behind her, so I was able to follow her in."

"Girl, you've got some balls! You followed her..."

Yolanda lifted her top and flashed her breasts at me again. "These the balls you're talkin' about, Holman?" she tugged her blouse and let it fall back into place. "Anyway, I went into her brother's office, not the inner office. I hung back and listened at the door once she was inside. She seemed to be giving him some sort of rundown about profits and losses. The, next thing I knew, it sounded like they were having sex in there!"

"Yo, you've got too much of an imagination. Bunny having sex with her brother? Are you sure there wasn't someone else in there? Maybe some other church deacon who she was meeting with, *that* I might believe."

"Well, I never actually *saw* who she was meeting with, I just assumed, you know, her brother's office, and all. It *did* have his name on the door."

"The Senator hired us because he thinks she's fooling around on him. It could well be she's having it off with one of her brother's employees. I think we need to get a few more hard facts settled before we offer any of this to the Senator. But collecting all that money? Are all the losers on the Texas coastal bend donating big bucks to a super mega church?"

"One other thing," my assistant said, picking up her handbag. "Naughty girl that I am, I stuck that little radio bug thing I found on e-Bay onto the undercarriage of Bunny's Lexus. So I can follow her where ever she goes on my *Iphone*, which is where I'm headed right now! Sorry Dave, guess it's beer and self-abuse for you tonight..."

"Be careful, Yo! I don't think we're dealing with nice folks here!"

CHAPTER FIVE

With her raven hair and dark eyes, Yolanda looks a little like that pop star, Cher. She often has that same mischievous look about her, like when Cher had just put one over on Sonny while they had the TV show. Beyond that, she could be a master of disguises. Sometimes she wore a little red dot on her forehead and a golden sari; she usually did that when she was raising funds for her elephant business. Other times, she might wear a tight gray flannel business number of blazer, blouse, skirt and stockings, or tee shirt and jeans. She looked good enough to eat in all her sundry outfits and, like a chameleon, easily blended with her surroundings. In her blond wig, which she had worn earlier in the day tailing the Senator's wife, she could be a California beach bunny who just copped a great tan, and sometimes, she could look so milk-toast plain you wouldn't notice her at all.

In spite of this, I always worried a little that she might come to harm. The lady was just too bold and overconfident. I never had an easy time of it when she took herself off on surveillance. But, on the other hand, I knew this lady was a natural. In the short time I'd been training her, she far surpassed me in stealth and blending skills.

Sipping Scotch and worrying, I must have nodded off in my chair. I was awoken by someone gently pulling the half-empty bottle from my hands. "Buy a girl a drink, sailor?"

Yolanda placed herself on my knee and took a long pull from the Cluny I'd been holding, then wrapped her arms, including the one holding the litre bottle, around my neck.

"You sober enough to hear my report, or should I go type it up for the morning?" She nudged my face around and laid a big wet kiss on me. "If that doesn't start your motor, I'll go turn on the computer."

"I'm here, Yo. What kind of night have you had?"

"Interesting," she gave with a rising inflection. "Bunny doesn't seem to have any lovers, but it might be better if that was what she had. She certainly seems to be well acquainted with the dregs of Corpus society!"

I raised my eyebrows, waiting for more.

"I followed her on a sweep around the worst neighborhoods you could find, down Agnes and Staples, through the projects and in the Hispanic area close to the old downtown. She made quite a few stops, what seemed like collection stops, to collect money would be my best guess, then she went on along the upper shore line. I don't think she was gathering church donations. On one corner, some guy in a cheap suit dragged a young girl in red and white striped stockings out of the doorway of an abandoned storefront. Two guys held her there while Mr. Suit had a chat with Bunny. When he'd spoken his piece, he tipped his head toward the girl and Bunny punched her hard in the gut. The girl fell forward and barfed her guts out, but then Bunny grabbed her by her hair, pulled her head back and kicked her in the face. The suit then tossed the kid into the gutter, kicked her himself. Bunny was smiling when she got back in her car and moved on.

"The evening ended up at the church, but I didn't hang around to see what went on there. Lights were on in the pastor's office, but it could have been anyone waiting there to collect Bunny's swag. I'd already seen enough to turn my stomach!"

I took a deep breath, then a large swallow of blended whiskey. "You think the Senator has any real clue about this?"

Yolanda made a thoughtful face. "I think maybe he's so caught up in his politics that he doesn't even notice she's gone until he wakes up in the night and she's not there.... He does seem the self-centered type."

I had to agree with that, spoiled and self-centered! Used to having everything handed to him and having his own way. Politicians were mostly power people. They assumed that everyone acknowledged their superior power and bowed down before them! Wives would gladly wait in line behind casual lovers just to share in all that power. But here, it seemed, was a wife with some mighty power of her own!

Did Bunny have other lovers, or was she just having orgasms wielding all this clout she carried? I'd have to give this some deep thought tomorrow. Right now, Yolanda was switching gears, tugging at my cargo shorts in a fashion I couldn't ignore. She was right, of course. I was just a typical, easily led, weak minded male.

CHAPTER SIX

I awakened the next morning to the smell of strong coffee. The way Yolanda brewed the stuff, a spoon would stand straight up in it! But it did pop my eyes open and get the old gray matter kicking over. I entered our small kitchen to find my partner at the stove sprinkling Sharwood's Hot Curry Powder over a skillet of scrambling eggs. There was already a platter of Nan bread on the table.

Yolanda was wearing skimpy green silk running shorts with yellow stripes down the sides and a tee shirt from the 2012 Rockport Art Festival. The short shorts made her naturally long and well sculpted legs look even longer. Her toe ring clicked on the hardwood floor as she brought our plates to the table in her bare feet.

Our digs were through a narrow door at the side of the office. Most people thought it was a closet. We shared two rooms and a low ceilinged kitchen that took up the rest of the upper story. When I rented the place, I figured it would just be me, and still found it a little cramped at that. After I met Yolanda and she chose to move in, she made the place seem a little larger to me. Kinda like two living more cheaply than one, I figured.

"I think someone in Gordon's church has a firm grasp on a share of Corpus Christi's organized crime," she announced without preamble as she sat, "maybe the Right Reverend himself. But definitely his sister has a hand in it."

"It's beginning to look that way. Maybe I should give Millar a call, see what he can tell me about vice along the bay front." Millar is a detective with the Corpus police force. I wouldn't exactly call him a friend, though we did have some friends in common. We shared a bit of mutual respect within a fat bubble of distrust. I'd shared some facts with him in the past that had cleared a double murder on his patch and we'd successfully worked together on a couple other cases of mutual interest. By my scorecard, Millar owed me one.

After breakfast I gave him a call, "Ken, ol' buddy, Holman here! Recovered any interesting bodies lately?"

"Your humor isn't that humorous, Holman. You want me to hang up and you can call back and try again?"

"Aw, don't hang up, Ken. I just want to pick your brains about something. Can I come by the station later this morning?"

"You think I want to be seen talking to a keyhole peeper? Right here in my own office? What do you need anyway?"

"I've got a few questions about whose running drugs and women around the bay front."

"So call somebody in vice, Holman. I'm kinda busy right now."

"Come on, Ken. I don't know anybody in vice. Help me out here!"

A hand covered the receiver for a few seconds, with just a handful of mumbles getting through. Then Ken came back on the line.

"How about lunch at the Iguana? That's in Portland, so nobody from here will have to know I'm cavorting with private heat. That's lunch for two of us on you, Holman. One of the vice guys is here with me right now and he's curious about why you'd be so curious. Make it 12:30. We've got a meeting in town first."

I started to say okay, but I was talking to a dial tone. Portland was just this side of Corpus Christi Bay, about half an hour away. That left me a couple hours. A beach walk would give me time to line my ducks up for presentation to the big city boys. A got on my bike and headed east for Rockport Beach.

There'd been a recent swarm of jellyfish, which littered the sand at the water's edge. I waded out in bay water up to my calves to avoid treading on the beached specimens. The ones still swimming were fewer in number and easier to avoid. Many of the jellies were cabbage heads, large opaque mushroom shapes that moved too sluggishly to prevent themselves from becoming beached.

In spite of the fishy obstacle course, my mind got into the zone pretty quickly. Why, I wondered, had the Senator really come to me in the first place? A man in his position could have used a large, bonded agency from Houston or San Antonio with much greater resources, not to mention an army of faceless operatives.

It could easily have just slipped the man's mind to tell me his wife was related to Reverend Clemson Gordon as he must have known I'd find that out quickly. Did Senator Jenkins have some suspicion or knowledge that his brother-in-law or his wife might be into something less than kosher?

And, I thought, there are a lot of things that could stifle a politician's chances. Was Jenkins really seeking something deeper, beyond an unfaithful wife, when he put me on the trail? So many questions!

I looked up to find I'd almost walked the full mile from the fishing pier, where I'd left my bike, to the Rockport jetty and I had only found more questions, no answers.

I waded deeper, skirting the rocky jetty that marked the west end of the beach, took my phone and wallet out of my pockets and held them over my head while I knelt down and immersed my body in the warm salty water. After a minute or two I stood, shook the water off my body like a dog might then turned to finish my walk back to my bicycle.

A hundred yards down the beach, I came on a sleek gray stingray coursing through the shallows. I bent down and asked the ray, "Do you have any answers little fellah?" The ray eyed me curiously for a heartbeat or two, then flipped to his right and turned back out to sea. I knew that American aboriginal natives regarded all animals as being signs with spirit messages to impart. "What do you symbolize, Mr. Manta," I said aloud, then continued along my watery path.

I reached my bike no wiser than when I had begun, so I peddled home, took a quick shower and picked out a fresh Hawaiian shirt. I chose one of my favorites, a custom made shirt from Moon Dog Shirt Company in Austin. The shirt was green and featured a repeating design of Thomas "Fats" Waller and Billy Holiday over a background of trad jazz players.

I gave Yolanda a goodbye peck on her forehead, where she sometimes wore that red dot. She squeezed my shoulders and told me to take care of myself. In spite of feeling totally clueless, I whistled an intricate bebop line as I took myself out to the car to drive to my meeting with Millar and his co-worker. Maybe I'd have an epiphany along the boring highway south.

The Iguana was two blocks off Highway 35 at the far end of Portland. It was a very comfortable mom-and-pop eatery that probably had the best Mexican food between Houston and the border. A dark unmarked Dodge Charger was parked out front. You'd never know it was a cop car if it wasn't for the 'tax exempt' license plates and the light trees in the front and back windows.

Ken Millar waved from the back corner of the room when I entered. He was sitting with a very tall and fit Hispanic man, salt-and-pepper hair, a bandito mustache and a clean white shirt. I sat down and Ken introduced me to Lieutenant Ralph Saldana, second in command of the Corpus Christi Vice Squad. It came to mind that I might have struck a nerve here.

The two cops were drinking dark beers and dipping corn chips into small bowls of salsa. Brushing bits of tortilla from his mustache, Saldana asked, "So what'd you want to talk to us about?" No beating about the bush here.

I answered Saldana's question with one of my own. "Have you seen any significant changes in illegal activity around the poor side of town lately?"

The two cops looked at each other. "Let's not be playing games here, Holman," Millar told me. "You must know something or you wouldn't be pulling our chains…. So what's going on?"

"Well… I've got this client who has asked me to follow his wife. He suspects her of cheating on him. Only the wife isn't seeing other men, she seems to be makin' the rounds of pimps and druggies. It looks like she's collecting money for someone…."

"I said don't beat around the bush, Holman. Let's have some names!"

"Client confidentiality," I told them, though my heart wasn't in it. I didn't want to drop the Senator's name, but I needed more information if I was going to help either him or myself.

Everyone was silent when the waitress came by and took our orders. The policemen ordered another round of beers and large combination plates. I indulged myself in a Cadillac margarita and an enchilada plate. As the girl walked towards the kitchen, my two guests remained tacit, focusing hard on their chips, salsa and beers.

"Holman," Millar cried shaking his head when the girl was a safe distance out of earshot. "We've got a serious upward trend in crime right now, *vice* type crime. Drugs and prostitution are on the rise. Someone is burning the old Mexican drug lords down, squeezing out the guys who we've been able to keep on a short leash for a lot of years. Whoever it is, they're ruthless and violent. Now, if you have any leads..."

I looked back and forth between the two serious cop faces. "I'm tailin' the wife of a politician. I can't name names you understand, but the way the wife is acting, I'm a little suspicious, that's all."

"So is this, uh, politician's wife on the game or something?"

"Ah, something like that," I improvised. "I need to see if I can rescue her, that's all."

"And if and when you do... are you going to keep us up to speed about what you learn?"

"Yes, of course! Only, if I knew just what I was getting into?"

"Oh, you're jumping into a big pit of fire," Saldana told me with a sly smile. "Since this little territory war started escalating, the murder rate in Corpus has nearly doubled. A lot of the dead are no real loss, people we've kinda wished would die or go away for some time now, but it's messing up our crime stats. The old chief was putting time in on the case himself as well as working with us to keep a lid on things, but since the chief crashed his motorcycle and died over in Port A, we've been having troubles. Now we suddenly got a lot more people lookin' at the department through a heavy spy glass."

I thought about it for a minute. "Well, I'm not one hundred percent sure... but it almost looks like the people my client's spouse is hanging with are sharing a lot of their ill gotten wealth with the Church of the Eternally Blinding Light, you know, that mega church..."

"We know the place, Holman," Saldana told me. "And if that's true, you'll have to gather some strong evidence against the place for us."

"Problem is, Holman," Millar cut in, "one of the deputy chiefs who's now temporarily in charge goes to that church, I think he's a deacon or some other high-up thing there, so the church is kinda off limits."

"A lot of other cops attend services there as well," Saldana added. "Many of them think ol' Pastor Gordon does a little walking on water himself. So any information you can give us would be strongly appreciated."

"I'll see what I can find. When I drove by to scope the place yesterday, some ugly little asshole in a vehicle sporting logos for

God's Security tried to roust me, so I'll have to be more careful next time."

"Be warned, Holman," Millar told me with a hollow laugh, "they've got surveillance cameras all over the grounds at that place. Gordon is a bit paranoid about Christian haters, Jews and homosexuals and a few other groups trying to infiltrate the place and desecrate it. That's the story we've been hearing anyway."

Saldana laughed as well. "The old chief wasn't even too welcome there, him being a gentleman of color, although no one ever told him that to his face."

"So these surveillance cameras," I asked, "there're mounted on the light poles around the grounds?"

"And the halls in most of the buildings," Saldana said, "Too many for anyone to effectively monitor, but enough to make your chances of entering and leaving the place unseen around one hundred to one."

"Thanks, Saldana, I'll keep that in mind…"

Then the girl was back with our meals. A young man accompanying her set our drinks in front of us. My two guests dug into their plates with gusto, having nothing further to say until their plates were nearly clean. As the young man who'd brought our drinks cleared the dishes away, the two plainclothesmen order more beer.

After a deep drink from his third beer, Saldana announced, "Pastor Clem Gordon, from what I've heard, isn't very fond of any 'brown types' either. He's a big campaigner for sealing the border and sending as many Mexicans 'home,' as he calls it, as they can catch. Personally, I can't stand the man!"

"I'm not that fond of him myself," Millar put forth. "I always suspected that the man is a hypocrite. If his church is in any way connected with our crime wave, or any other illegal activities, I'd be more than happy to bring him down. But we'd need a lot of help, probably Texas Rangers from outside the area. I've heard Gordon has a big following with a lot of cops from the surrounding areas as well. Especially in Port Aransas, where he lives."

"He lives in Port Aransas?"

"Yeah," Saldana told me. "He's got a compound over there that's bigger than many of the area's housing developments. It's set behind high walls on three sides. The state doesn't allow anything built on the dunes, so instead of a wall, he has a small army manning trenches all along the beachfront. He's got two sets of gates you have to pass through to get in, one outside the wall and another just inside. Some of the guys in the department work security for him part time, is how we know all this. His compound security is said to be tighter than the borders around Israel!"

Millar brought his wrist up and looked at his watch. Looking at his partner, he said, "Ralph, we get off in another hour, at three, and I've got some paperwork on my desk to go through..."

"Yeah, it's time to vamoose from this joint. Thanks for the lunch, Holman. And keep in touch. Saldana held out a business card. "My personal cell number is on the back. If you've got something good, call me anytime, twenty-four seven!"

CHAPTER SEVEN

When I got back to the office, Yolanda had a plastic bag of clothing on my desk that she was going through. It looked like some kind of rag picker's stash. "I've been shopping at Castaways," she announced.

Castaways is a big thrift shop just down the block from the office. Their sales lent support to a dozen or more local churches here in Rockport. Even with the proceeds of this supermarket size project, none of the local churches were even one third the size of Clem Gordon's Church of the Eternally Blinding Light.

"What, you *bought* this crap?"

"Ten bucks for the whole bag," she smiled.

On the table was an old cotton house dress, something like my mother might have worn back in the fifties. A flower-patterned garment that looked old enough to actually have been from that time. There was also a colorful cotton head scarf, a set of rosary beads and a bright red, green and yellow woven serape-style jacket. Yolanda pulled a pair of pink high top tennis shoes from the bag, then pushed it aside.

"The other night, when I was tailing the Senator's wife, I noticed a beat up old van parked by the main church building. I checked it through my binoculars. The fading logo on the side said Arista's Cleaning Service. There were maybe a dozen Mexican women with brooms, mops and pails piling into the vehicle. I did some research on the Internet this morning while you were out.

Arista's has a shady reputation, but they're about the cheapest firm out there to clean office buildings. The site I checked on the net warns that the crews are all illegals making less than seven dollars a *night*. The company is bonded, but there are no background checks on the people they hire. One comment on the website I was viewing said that a manager in one of their client's offices talked to one of the maids while he was working late. After interviewing the women and one of her co-workers, he found that they were being kept like slaves in a condemned hotel outside Robstown. When he asked one of the girls why she didn't run away, the woman told the interviewer that if she didn't behave herself and work hard, her two children back in Mexico would be tortured and killed. Gordon's church appears to be Arista's biggest client after a couple used car dealerships and an old shoreline office building. There are other comments from businesses that used to use them but let them go after things were going missing from the premises."

"And you're going to donate some old clothes to one of these workers?" I sneered.

"I'm going to *be* one of the workers," Yolanda grinned. "Thinking about the cleaning service, I devised a plan to have a look at some of the church records. I'll drive your car down there around 9:00 tonight, when the cleaning crew arrives, park a few blocks away and sneak onto the property. If I can mingle with the ladies as they leave the van, I'll find a way to get into the office and have a quick look through the files. I'll bring that little James Bond cigarette lighter camera thing of yours and maybe even get some pictures."

"Not approved! You'll end up getting rounded up with the others and next thing you know, *you'll* be living in that Robstown hotel. It's a totally hair brained scheme, Yo! I can't let you do it."

"Ah, come on, Dave! You know I can handle myself." She stood and posed a bad karate stance as she blew another pink gum bubble. She popped the bubble for a sound effect as she brought the flat of her hand down through the air miming breaking a board or a brick or something, "Besides, I plan to sneak out of church long before they finish cleaning the place. I'll be wearing dark tights and a black leotard under my maid's outfit. I'll ditch the clothes and sneak back to your car and be home before midnight. No one will ever know…"

"Yo, I was told they have video cameras all over that property. You truly believe no one will see you? They might already have you on a security video from last night! You'll be taking a big chance."

"They might *see* me, but they'll never catch up with me." She blew another gum bubble, popped it and scraped some bubble residue off her pretty nose. "I run swift like Bengal tiger, B'wana!"

"I don't know, Yo. I'm not keen on this!"

"Well, I'm doing it anyway. Dave, the firm already has ten bucks invested in my costume.…"

CHAPTER EIGHT

I've found it's impossible to argue with Yolanda when her mind is made up. I waved goodbye to her just after 7:30, then came back up to the office, mixed a pitcher of gin and tonic and worried about her while I drank. It was weird to think that this kid, who I've known less than a year, meant more to me than either of my ex-wives ever had.

I got up to add another squeeze of lime to my jug of booze and discovered Yolanda had left a small pot of Biryani rice on the back of the stove for me. When did I suddenly develop this craving for hot Indian food? I was raised a Minnesota meat and potatoes man. I ate the rice right out of the pot with a tablespoon, then set the dish aside, leaned back and put my feet on my desk.

It was just after midnight when laughter on the stairs brought me out of my alcoholic haze. My assistant came into the room with a big grin and an excited air. Skulking around always seemed to get her motor started. She parked herself on my lap and took a drink of gin straight from the pitcher.

"I got it, Dave! Got photos of documents connecting Gordon to drugs, hookers, lap dancers and more! Would you believe the church owns three 'gentlemen's clubs' in Corpus? It was, how you say, a piece of cake!"

My girl was still dressed in her dark top and tights. She had some grease paint on her face, but light glinted off her bright red toe nail polish and the silver ring on her bare foot. Her dark hair hung straight as a horse's tail down her back where it was still partially tucked into the top of her leotard.

"We can develop the film in the morning, Dave. You know how hot this kind of detective work makes me. Right now I just want to throw you down in bed and have my wicked way with you!"

"Or vice versa," I laughed. "Remember, I'm the man here!"

Yolanda gave a wicked wink, "If you say so, B'wana!" She was already pulling her leotard over her head as she sat on my knee.

Despite the smell of waiting coffee, I was in the bathroom with the red light burning, moving film from the developer to the fixing solution balanced atop our small bathroom sink. When I moved the thin strip of cellulose to the enlarger and turned on the light, I could see that Yolanda's images were clear and sharp. Many of the squares showed pages from a ledger, a few were notebook covers and the remaining images looked like contracts or agreements signed by employees of the church.

"I tried to get what looked to be most important." Yolanda told me as I came from our bathroom turned darkroom with a handful of black and white eight by tens. "I knew I only had so much time…."

"I'd say you did very well," I complimented her. "Now the question is, do we take these straight to Millar and Saldana or do we give the Senator a 'heads up' first?"

"The Senator *is* our client," Yolanda gave me in her most serious tone. "I don't like the man, but he's holding the checkbook."

"I'll call the Senator right after breakfast," I promised. "You can scan the photos into the computer and make backup copies."

"Oops," my lady told me. "We're out of laser photo paper. You'll have to drive to that office supply place in Aransas Pass and get some more. Wouldn't hurt to get another couple cartridges of ink as well."

CHAPTER NINE

After eating, I called the Senator, only to learn he was in a series of meetings in Austin this morning. His aide promised he would call me back as soon as he was free, so I took off for Aransas Pass.

I probably could have bought what we needed at the local Rockport Walmart, but I didn't like shopping there. I didn't like the Walton family's attitude or the fact that they were the richest family in America, so I headed for the only mom and pop office supply store I knew of.

I had only been on the road for a couple minutes. Traffic was very light, not another car in sight. Passing the Highway 188 Sinton exit, I noticed a pair of large white sport utility vehicles sitting by the onramp. When I topped the bridge over Highway 188, the first vehicle bounded up the onramp to cut me off with inches to spare. When I stood on my brakes, the other truck sped up behind me and to my left, sliding sidewise to block any chance of my backing up. Before I had time to evaluate what was going on, men in dark suits and hoods poured forth from both vehicles and took a stance by the doors of my old Saab. I reached up to hit the door lock on my side, but the door was torn open before I got my hand up to the window sill. I cursed myself for not having a newer car with automatic central locking.

Gloved hands roughly grabbed me and pulled me from my car. I was thrown to the gravel where someone placed a foot on my back. Another of the men knelt down and laced plastic ties around my wrists and ankles then lifted me like a rag doll into the back of one of the big trucks. As I was being pulled up from the ground, out of the corner of my eye I saw another man getting into my Saab as it started rolling towards the watery ditch at the side of the highway.

My prison truck drove for what seemed like a long time. Face down on the floor I could only guess where they might be taking me. I lost track of the number of turns we made. The smooth highway was eventually replaced by a potholed track, then a gravel path that threw up small stones at the undercarriage.

The vehicle stopped briefly. The driver got out and there was some shouting, then we advanced a few more feet. I was soon roughly pulled up to my knees and then out of the truck by my wrist ties. The plastic bit deeply into my flesh as I was being tossed around. We were in a ramshackle old barn that seemed to be leaning precariously, as through it was about to collapse in on itself. Weeds grew tall and wild through cracks in the concrete floor. My captors carelessly dropped me into an old cane back chair and laced a short rope around me to hold me there.

Hoods came off, not a good omen for me leaving this place alive. I saw that one of my kidnappers was the man from God's Security who had stopped to lecture me earlier in the week. He shot me a wide grin, then kicked me hard in the shin of my left leg and laughed manically.

"God don't like you much, son!" he cackled.

Shortly after that, all the men in the group put on very serious faces and took up stations in a square around my chair. A door creaked behind me and I heard shuffling feet. Then Pastor Clem

Gordon was standing before me aiming a sour look my way. In person, he looked even fatter than he appeared on television. The man had to weigh in around four-hundred pounds!

"Well, well... Welcome Mr. Lindstrom. Or is it Mr. Holman? I'm a little confused here. I seem to be getting some crossed signals from somewhere and the lord ain't speakin' to me to help me out much in this.

"So, are you E.B. Lindstrom or David Holman? If you're not sure, maybe I can help jog your memory a little." He reached in the pocket of a sort of suede car coat he was wearing and brought forth an ugly little gray instrument, pushed a button on it and blue sparks shot forth, a cattle prod.

I flinched back as much as I could in my trussed up position and he laughed. "So what's your interest in my church, Mr. Holman? I don't think you came by there seeking salvation. Frankly, I don't think you're the Lord's kinda guy, Holman, so what is it?" He touched the small device to my upper arm, knocking me back on the chairs rear legs with a jolt of strong current.

I shook my head violently to try and clear my brain. "I'm helping out your brother-in-law, Senator Jenkins," I breathed heavily at him. "He thinks his wife, your sister, has been cheating on him. He's afraid that if the public thinks she needs other men or is possibly going to leave him, he won't get re-elected. As a man of the cloth you know how important marital fidelity is in this state!"

The Right Reverend hauled back and punched me hard in the gut. As my upper body pitched forward from the blow, he delivered a right cross deep into my face. The world seemed to swim before me for a few beats. There were stars circling in front of my eyes and blood began trickling from my nose. Gordon thought this was hilarious, nearly doubling over with laughter now.

Just as quickly as the laughter had come, his face was dead straight again. "Why should ol' Burt Jenkins think my sister would be cheating on him? And why should he care? The way that man jumps from bed to bed…. And I didn't know he even paid that much attention to what Elizabeth Anne might be doin'."

"Well, I guess he got some kind of wild hair. He told me something is going on and hired me to find out what. That's all I know…"

The pastor punched me again, throwing my head around and loosening one of my teeth. "I don't know if I believe you, Holman." He was shaking his head. "And just how much did he tell you about the history of him and my sister anyway?"

"He didn't give me any background!" I spoke too loudly through my broken mouth. Then more quietly, I said, "He just paid me to find some answers and then try to fix things so his wife doesn't cost him the election!"

"I've got a lot invested in our boy the Senator," Gordon said with a thoughtful pose. "*I'll* make sure Elizabeth Anne behaves. He doesn't need no private eye snooping around to guarantee that, and I don't need you peeping around in my business either, Holman. Now you go on and be a good boy, behave yourself and tell Burt that it's all taken care of and Elizabeth Anne won't cost him any votes. Tell him he doesn't require your services anymore, is that clear?" The last three words were shouted, half an octave higher than the first part of the sentence, then the Reverend's voice returned to normal.

"And, if I ever catch you snoopin' around my business again, we might just have to bob that little ol' trunk of yours..." He poked two stiff fingers into my crotch, "so you won't be able to satisfy your little nigger elephant girl anymore." He shook his head, sending his white pompadour flying into a parody of Donald Trump's hair before he delivered a look of purest pity my direction. "Jesus loves me," he chuckled, "but he cain't stand you!"

As if on cue, all the heavies gathered around the room joined him bursting into laughter of their own. Clemson walked towards the building's side door and the others fell into a sort of formation to follow him out.

They left a box cutter sitting on the back of the seat behind me. It took me an hour or so, but I eventually got my numb fingers around it and managed to saw through the plastic ties on my wrists, then I cut the bonds on my ankles. My Saab was parked outside the barn with the key in the ignition, but I had no clue as to where I was. I followed the path from the barn to a two-lane road. The setting sun clued me which direction was west, so I turned to the east. Eventually, I came out to Highway 44, just past Corpus Christi International Airport. I had to stop for gas at a convenience store in North Beach on my way home, and got quite a look from the young girl at the counter when I paid for my gas and a quart can of Miller beer. She touched her own face as though it hurt in sympathy with mine, but she took my money and didn't say anything.

Walking into the office a little after 10:00, Yolanda looked up and ran to throw her arms around me. I could feel her tears on my face as she held it against mine.

"Oh, Dave, oh Dave," she mumbled it over and over again as she led me back to our apartment and retrieved the first aid kit from the bathroom medicine cabinet.

CHAPTER TEN

I don't know how she got them, but Yolanda produced a small vial of super painkillers that knocked me out until almost noon the next day. My jaw was swollen and my tooth still loose enough to wiggle around a little, but I felt much better as I sat up and ate the boiled egg she brought me with little toast soldiers and some of her strong coffee. After breakfast, Yolanda crawled back under the sheets with me and just held me for a long while.

Yolanda lying next to me, with my arm around her, we reviewed what we knew of the case so far. The Senator suspected his wife, but hadn't been paying much attention to her or her movements. It was only with an election coming up that he became concerned about her lifestyle. That was problem number one. Then there was Clemson Gordon, another power mad individual who exercised a lot of control over Senator Jenkins using both money and, it appeared, his sister, the Senator's wife. Did the Senator have any clue where his brother-in-law or his church were getting their money? And if he knew, would he really be that concerned? He had stated more than once that getting reelected was all he really cared about.

"What would Sam Spade do?" I joked.

"Or Boston Blackie, or Phillip Marlowe?" Yolanda added with a giggle.

I put on my finest Bogart impression, "Sweetheart, if I was Marlowe, I'd have to find all the dames in this thing and sleep with them, one at a time, until they led me to the answers."

Her giggles stopped abruptly. She rolled away from me and sat straight up in the bed, her dark eyes burning right through me. "Just remember, Holman, you ever fool around on me, I'll cut your dick off and send it back to you in one of those cute little gift wrap boxes from Beall's."

With that, she got up and went out to the office. The bumbling Italian captain from a British TV comedy I liked flashed into my brain saying, "What-a mistake-a to make-a!"

The Senator returned my call from the day before just after two in the afternoon. I invited him around to the office. I told him I'd give him a report to keep him up to date, and also that there were a few things I needed to discuss with him.

"I'm pressed for time right now, Holman. Just give me the Reader's Digest short version and send me the report."

"It's a bit complicated," I told him. "We really need to sit down and have a private little téte-a-téte."

The Senator grumbled and hemmed and hawed, but finally agreed to meet with me in half an hour at the Poor Man's Country Club, a two story, barn-like saloon on the main highway that faced Little Bay and the wealthy neighborhoods on Key Allegro.

The familiar white Lincoln was parked behind the Poor Man's Country Club with the engine running and the air conditioning turned up high. The driver rolled his window down and pointed to the barn-like structure. "The Senator is waiting inside, on the second deck patio." I parked my bicycle against the fence and went through the side door. Crossing the room, I noticed a waitress coming down the stairs and asked her to send a Dos Equis to the Senator's table for me.

Up the stairs and outside on the deck, the Senator sat by himself. No one else was around in spite of the fact that it was almost happy hour in the bar. The man appeared nervous, fidgeting with the lime on the rim of his drink and turning his head to and fro to check who else might be close enough to hear us. The girl came out and put my bottle on the table, smiled and left.

"So, what's so important that we had to see each other face to face, Holman?" He raised his head toward the sky as if checking for microphones that might be dangling overhead. "And what the hell happened to your face?"

"A couple of reasons for the meeting," I told him without a smile. "First off, your brother-in-law assures me that there is no problem. He says his sister is ever faithful to you and that if she isn't, he'll talk with her and make sure that she is. He wants me to drop your case. He says all this is a misunderstanding on your part. And while he was tellin' me all this, he delivered a few playful punches. That's why my nose and lips are bit swollen."

"That self-important son-of-a-bitch," the Senator shouted, then checking himself, added in a softer voice, "He doesn't know anything about my private life! He might wish he did, but...."

"The Right Reverend wanted to know how much you've told me about the history of your relationship with..."

"That's not important, Holman!" He hissed. "What matters is what is going on right now, what that woman is up to *right now!*"

"Well, what's going on right now," I told him bluntly, "is that your wife seems to be involved in some criminal activity along the sleazy side of Corpus Christi. I had her tailed and she made a tour of the underbelly of the city collecting money from criminals; prostitutes, drug dealers and the like."

"Bullshit, Holman! You just want to smear my wife to get me out of office and keep me out. I never should have come to a liberal son-of-a-bitch like you for help. Damn you!" He started to rise out of his chair. I pushed him back down with two fingers and stood over him.

"Just listen to me, Senator. Your wife is dirty, that's a documented fact. I think she's working for her brother. And I have photos. I believe that criminal activity has more to do with supporting Gordon's church than the Faithfull's tithing does. I've been talking with a vice detective with the Corpus cops. Something is rotten in your brother-in-laws church!"

"That's it, Holman. You're fired! Not another penny from me and if you used any of this to try and discredit me, I'll see that you're run out of the great state of Texas in disgrace!"

"Senator," I offered in my most soothing tone. "I think you need to take this seriously. I am on *your* side and I'm trying to help you. I'm looking for a way to expose your brother-in-law without dragging your wife into it. You want to win. I don't really care if you win or not, but my job right now is to solve your problems so you'll at least have the *chance* to win. I'm working for you and I'll do whatever I can, whatever it takes to clear this up for you."

Senator Burt Jenkins slipped down farther into his chair, sucked up half the liquid in his glass and regarded me with eyes that could win a hand of poker. His breathing calmed as he thought about my words.

"I cain't help but like you, Holman, you're a likable guy. And I'd like to trust you too. So what makes you think Clemson's church is dirty and just how much do you have on Bunny?"

I thought for a minute, pondering just where to begin and how to form words that the Senator might hear without taking offense or jumping to half true conclusions. The waitress appeared in the doorway. The Senator pointed a fat finger at his glass to signal that he needed a refill. I hadn't touched my beer yet.

"I had someone sneak into Gordon's office. My operative went through some files and took pictures of a set of books that show profits from drugs sales, sex for sale and possibly extortion as well. I haven't shared any of these photos yet, but I'll have to give copies to Lieutenant Saldana of the Corpus Christi cop shop pretty quick.

"Your brother-in-law told me he'll make sure his sister, ah, behaves is how he put it. I don't know if that means he's going to stop using her as a bagman, or just that he's going to tell her to be more careful. Anyway, I'm going to keep an eye on your wife for another day or two. If it looks like she's out of the picture, I'll give my evidence to the Corpus cops and keep her out of it. I'll see that they give her some protection as well, as a favor to you."

"And if she keeps on bein' visible in these criminal activities?"

"Well then, Senator, I'll have to see what I can do to get her out of there. I may need you to send her away somewhere for a little time while the cops investigate Clem Gordon. Maybe she could take a vacation to Paris or Hawaii."

"You sayin' kidnap my own wife? How is that gonna look?"

"If you want to remain a viable candidate, you'll just have to talk with her. You need to get her cooperation, at least until after the election. By that time, hopefully, the police can sort out whatever bad element is working within Gordon's church and get it all tied up. Once the church is cleaned up, your Bunny should be in the clear and she won't be a threat. The two of you can get some private counseling or whatever it takes to save your marriage."

"Alright, Holman, you're still on the case. And I apologize f' losin' my temper. I'm puttin' a hell of a lot of faith in you, Holman. Don't you dare let me down now!"

CHAPTER ELEVEN

Walking out of the bar, I noticed the white God's Security car sitting across the highway on a small patch of gravel by Little Bay. As I watched, the window rolled down and the nasty little man who had stopped me a few days before gave a small wave, then raised the glass back into the hole. Was he tailing me or was he watching the Senator? I didn't want to seem paranoid. It could be either of us.

Riding my bike through the back streets towards Market Street, I glanced often over my shoulder, but no one seemed to be following me. There was no God's Security vehicle waiting when I arrived at the office. I decided that Reverend Gordon was just verifying that I was meeting with the Senator. Hopefully, they would assume I was meeting him to officially take myself off the case. I'd have to be much more careful about being seen with the Senator in the future.

Back in the office I fixed myself a drink and thought about what my next move should be. The Corpus Police, I decided. Now that the Senator was in the picture I had no excuse to withhold evidence. I brought copies of Yolanda's photographs out of the filing cabinet and put them in a clean, white nine by eleven envelope. On a wild whim, I parted the dusty blinds with my fingers to look out at the road. God's Security was out there. He was parked some distance down the road, but close enough to let me know he was keeping an eye on me. I made a call to Detective Saldana and arranged a quick meeting to bring him the copies of the documents Yolanda had photographed at the church, then I left a note for my girl and snuck out the back window of our flat. I crept across the building's back roof and slid down one of the rusting support poles of the feed store's storage area. The store stood between me and Market Street, blocking the security man's view of my movements as I disappeared through the adjacent 1069 RV Park. I circled around through the neighborhood eventually coming out on Business Route 35. I walked down the four-lane, crossing Market Street behind my watcher and continued on a couple blocks farther to the Enterprise Car Rental Agency.

At Enterprise, I rented a sub-compact something, a light blue snub-nosed car with air conditioning, a radio and not much else. The drive to Portland took about forty minutes and Saldana was waiting outside the Whataburger there in a black pick-up that must have been his own personal vehicle.

The vice cop got out of his truck and motioned me to follow him into the air conditioned burger joint. We both ordered coffee and took a booth by the front window.

"Bunny Jenkins, so your client has to be the Senator," Saldana began with serious eyes after blowing on his paper cup and taking a small sip.

I didn't say anything, so he added, "Pretty simple deduction, Holman. I had some guys I trust scope out the scene from a distance. They pulled an all-nighter in a borrowed Time Warner Cable van, photographing all the players where drugs change hands or old men crawl along the curbs. Bunny Jenkins stood out there like a festering ingrown toenail. You know that her brother is Clemson Gordon, don't you?"

"Okay, Saldana, you've got me. Yes, I know about the family connections...."

"So I had my guys put a tail on Bunny Jenkins the next night," "She certainly seems to know a few suspicious types out there. We couldn't get any pictures of money changing hands, but it looked like she was making pickups and exchanges, even playing the enforcer. She seemed to be getting off on this stuff!

"At one point, my officers said they really wanted to bust her. She pulled a gun on some poor teenager and made the girl give one of her fat greasy heavies a blowjob. I had, however, told my men that the drill was observe only. But they did get photographs of that assault. They are hoping they can arrest her at some point and use their pictures in evidence. These guys have daughters, and they take shit like this seriously."

"I promised the Senator that I would keep his old lady out of it if at all possible...."

"That might not be easy, Holman. So what have you got for me?"

I set the envelope on the table. He turned back the flap and withdrew the black and white eight by tens. The man took his time, carefully examining each shot. At a couple, he seemed to hold his breath, then let it out slowly.

"If only I had more people I could trust on our force, we could have this guy in a matter of days. As it is, I'm afraid this evidence would disappear from sight as quickly as I logged it in. I don't like the word corruption, Holman. I just think too many folks in the department believe a holy light shines out of this man's ass. And that light is likely to blind them to the truth, that the man is a phony and a criminal, hell, a captain of crime...organized crime!"

"So what can we do?" I asked him. "Gordon has a guy outside my office watching me. Yesterday, the Reverend himself had me kidnapped. He punched me around a little and then told me to drop the Senator as a client and leave him and his business alone."

"I was curious where you got those bruises, but I don't imagine you want to press charges."

"I want to see that man take the needle, Saldana. Nothing less! But I want to try and keep my word to the Senator as well. I promised Jenkins I'd keep his wife out of this and keep it a few degrees away from his re-election campaign."

"That isn't going to be an easy job," Saldana told me shaking his head. "I know a Texas ranger who I trust to do the right thing. I spoke with him earlier this morning. I'll give these photos to him after making a back-up copy for myself. He's promised to put together a task force in secret, some of our men who I trust along with some county boys and staties. He knows the Senator, but I'm not sure if he likes the man. I'll ask him to try and spare Bunny Jenkins if we can."

"Thanks, Saldana. In the meantime, I'll try and find out more of what's going on there. I have a female assistant who's on the case with me. She's a master of disguises and pretty good at surveillance as well. I might just have to sit back and keep God's Security busy while she does the legwork."

CHAPTER TWELVE

Back in Rockport, I parked the rental heap on Apple Street, the next lane over behind my office. I tiptoed through the trailers at the RV Park. I thought about shinnying up the post and climbing back in the bedroom window, but dismissed that as too much work. If Clemson Gordon's little man sees me walking up the stairs, he'll probably just think he missed me going down to the feed store for a coke or something.

Yolanda was busy at her computer. "I'm checking backgrounds on some of the members of Gordon's church," she spoke without turning he head. "There are some interesting people on his roster."

"Where did you get a list of Gordon's congregation, Yo?"

"Everything's on the Internet if you know where to look, Dave." She took a sip of tea from a mug resting near her keyboard, then turned her lovely head to give me a smile. "You really need to learn how to use a computer."

"Aren't those files protected by passwords or something?"

Yolanda giggled. "Gordon *does* have his stuff password protected. I got it on the second try. It's susej evol, love jesus spelled backwards. What a simpleton!"

I brought my chair over and sat by Yolanda's desk. We perused a few dozen of the dossiers on church deacons and major donors, only it looked like the donors were probably getting a good return on their investment. Gordon might not like brown types, but he had quite of few of them in his hierarchy, along with a number of recent Russian immigrants of questionable character. Their addresses were spread out from Houston all the way to Reynosa, with very few local Corpus Christi residents. Police officers were marked with an LE coding. We figured that out first. After a lot of discussion, Yolanda convinced me that the MAph code most likely stood for methamphetamines; drug lab owners or dealers. That accounted for most of the Spanish sir names and half the Russians. By nightfall, we had four different lists, separated according to different illegal vices. Some names appeared on more than one list, but most the names on our criminal lists seemed well divorced from the roles of the average church goers.

Just before midnight, Yolanda printed out our findings in triplicate so we'd have one copy for the cops, one to give to Senator Jenkins and one for our own files. She told me she was exhausted as she powered down her computer, but she came very much alive when we turned back the sheets!

CHAPTER THIRTEEN

A ringing phone woke me up. It was still dark outside and the ring tone was unfamiliar. Was I dreaming? I wandered out into the office in my tee shirt and y-fronts to find Yolanda on her special phone, the one reserved for her non-profit game, her elephant line. Maybe a relative was calling from India? What was the time difference and what time might it be right now in Asia?

Yolanda tilted her head toward the legal pad on my desk, putting her hand over the receiver and mouthing "pen and paper." She began taking notes as she listened, the phone held against her ear with her shoulder. Her neat and precise script was easy to read, but wasn't making any sense to me. "Three Rivers," she wrote, then underlined it three times. After that she added. "Starving, maybe ill," and "Bar None," which she also underlined.

Was the Senator's wife in trouble? And if so, why would someone call on an obscure 800 number that advertised rescuing elephants? I crossed my arms over my chest and waited for Yolanda to end the call.

When she had hung up the instrument, she looked into my inquisitive face and said, "That was an anonymous caller. They wanted to report an elephant emergency." My expression must have turned even more confused.

"Some rich bastard bought his kids a pet elephant," she scowled. "Apparently it was fun for awhile, then the kids got tired of it and moved on to other interests. They stopped feeding it and playing with it. I guess the ranch hands got tired of cleaning up after it as well. We need to get out there. It's a place called the Bar None Ranch, just outside Three Rivers. The caller said its a few miles west of Lake Corpus Christi."

"Wait a minute," I stated in amazement. "You mean this elephant rescue thing is *for real*!"

Yolanda gave me a hurt look and put on her sing-song Indian accent. "Dave, did you think I was playing at some kind of scam? Of course my elephant rescue is real! Elephants are very sensitive creatures, and we Indian girls love elephants. Someone has to look out for these wonderful animals."

"But, there aren't any elephants in Texas, I mean outside of the zoos, are there? I just thought…"

"Things are not always as they seem, Dave. Obviously there is at least *one* elephant here, and right now it needs our help!"

She picked up the elephant line telephone and began dialing. I had to answer the call of nature, so I went back to the apartment. When I came into the office again, Yolanda announced, "My uncle Jishnu is flying down here from New York. He is organizing our rescue team and they'll be driving down… from Houston, I think."

She got some coffee going and then went back into the apartment. I toasted some bread and was spreading it with peanut butter when she came back out. Yolanda was wearing a yellow sari with little red designs on it. She had once again placed the small red dot on her forehead.

"This is serious business." she told me. "We must put everything else on hold temporarily. Jishnu's private plane will be flying into Rockport Fulton airport around 11:00 and I will drive out to meet him."

I was introduced to Yolanda's uncle on the fly. She called on her cell phone from the airport and told me that I should be ready to go and waiting outside, by the road, in ten minutes. They would pick me up, but there was no extra time for Uncle Jishnu to come up to our place or make nice. Our schedule was tight.

Yolanda was driving and a dark little man dressed in what looked like white pajamas that I assumed was her uncle rode shotgun. I scrunched my bulk into the tiny back seat. There was no legroom at all, so I sat sideways with my feet on the seat. As we pulled onto Highway 35 headed toward Corpus, one of the white God's Security vehicles with the eye and scarlet cross on the door fell in behind us and stayed on our tail until we turned west on U.S. 181, just outside Gregory. I kept an eye out after that, but didn't spot any other suspicious cars or trucks. At Sinton, we pulled onto State Highway 181, heading toward Lake Corpus Christi. A few miles along, we were overtaken by a large U-Haul stake truck, which pulled in front of us and slowed. Uncle Jishnu gave the truck a 'thumbs up' and then said something to Yolanda that I couldn't make out over the roar of the wind. Yolanda turned briefly and shouted, "Our team!"

Just short of Three Rivers, we exited south onto Highway 72, where our caravan was joined by a red and white compact car that advertised Live Oak County Constable on the door. We let the constable take the lead and followed him off on a side road, and then a gravel track beneath a gate with the Bar None brand and logo hanging above. Just short of the large sprawling house, we saw the shaded corral where the small pachyderm lay on its side in the dirt so weak it looked like it would barely be able to stand.

The U-Haul truck driver pulled up as close to the pen as he could and three dark complexioned young men hopped out; two of them cuddling the poor pachyderm, one of them gently stroking its forehead, while the third man brought a brown satchel from the truck, opened it and proceeded to check the creature's vital signs.

Yolanda parked at the side of the drive and quickly ran back to join them. I followed, and she introduced the fellows. Payush and Butthead were grad students in Houston who had volunteered to help any way they could. The third man, Darpaknu was a veterinary assistant in Richland, also a volunteer. Butthead, they told me, was really named Budhan, but Americanized his name after seeing the famous cartoon character on television.

As Darpaknu examined the young elephant, Payush and Budhan filled a big bowl with fresh water and found the bag of feed in a nearby shed to give the creature sustenance. After a thorough examination, Darpaknu proclaimed the young pachyderm to be in fairly good health, but suffering from depression as well as malnutrition.

The constable had gone ahead to the main house where he first spoke to some ranch hands. He demanded to speak to the ranch owner himself, who finally came out, short tempered and curious as to why all these people were trespassing on his land. He windmilled his arm and gave angry glares at the constable, but finally calmed down.

I walked up to the big house to listen to their conversation. The rancher's concern was for the money he'd spent more so than for the animal's life.

"I was on safari in Africa," the rancher told the constable. "A couple of local tribesmen had this baby elephant. They'd killed the mother for her tusks, but thought the baby was worth something. Hell, the thing would'a died if I hadn't crated it up and brought it home with me! I thought it might make a nice pet for my kids... something none of the other kids had. I didn't realize how much care the damn thing needed, and the kids didn't want the responsibility. What the hell, the animal only lived as long as it did because I took it out of Africa!"

Uncle Jishnu offered the cowboy a substantial check in compensation, I couldn't believe the figure. This elephant rescue thing was serious business! Jishnu and the man dickered for a short time, but finally came to an agreement. When I returned to the corral, the young Indian men had helped the baby elephant into a bed of straw on the back of the stake truck. Budhan was snuggled up with the young animal, his arms around the creature stroking his belly. The other two were in the cab anxious to get on the road.

We made our preparations to leave and the constable went back to the rancher and wrote the man a ticket for animal abuse. The cowboy exploded, turning red and shouting, but the officer assured him it was no joke. He was still shouting about lawyers and congressmen as we exited his property. Was Jenkins his Senator, I wondered?

The sun was low on the horizon when we got back to Rockport. The young men put the elephant into one of the corrals behind the feed store where my office is. Then they pitched a large tent back in the trees behind the property, near the adjacent trailer park. Uncle Jishnu came upstairs and had dinner with us, Yolanda preparing an especially hot crab vindaloo using local Rockport blue crab.

"When the baby is stronger," Yolanda announced, in maybe a week, the boys will be taking her to Tennessee. Uncle Jishnu has arranged to send the animal to the Elephant Sanctuary, America's largest elephant habitat, a park in Hohenwald, Tennessee." She smiled at the small brown man who was her uncle.

"They have excellent veterinary care there and acres for the elephants to roam around the park," the uncle chimed in. "And there are many other elephants. I have seen this myself!" Then he added, "Elephants are very social creatures, you know. They need company of their own kind!"

"I thought this was all a joke," I replied in amazement, "this elephant rescue thing."

"I assure you sir, this is a real and very important charity," Uncle Jishnu told me shaking his head.

"But we don't really have elephants in Texas!"

"Things are not always what they seem, Holman!" Yolanda repeated again.

The three young helpers came up later to join us for coffee. They reminisced with my girl about a petting zoo in McKinney they had busted the year before, saving the lives of three Indian elephants.

"That was before I met you, Dave," she smiled. "You will learn that this was not the only elephant in Texas."

CHAPTER FOURTEEN

U ncle Jishnu stayed for breakfast, but told us he needed a ride to the airport right away when he'd swallowed the last bite of his food. Yolanda filled a thermos of her strong coffee for him to drink on his private plane then followed him down to the VW Thing. God's Security was still parked down the road, but the vehicle's driver appeared to be asleep behind the lightly tinted windows.

I sat at my desk with a yellow legal pad and Yolanda's internet lists of church members trying to connect some meaningful dots. I hoped someone on the police task force would be better at it than I was.

Yolanda was back within the hour. She kissed the top of my head in passing. After wiping the red dot from her forehead and changing back into cut-off jeans and one of my flamingo covered Hawaiian shirts, she went straight to her computer. After a lot of mouse clicking action, I heard her snort, then chuckle and then she loudly hollered "Bingo!"

I pushed up from my chair and rushed to look over her shoulder, but again, I saw just an ambiguous computer screen with a woman's photo in one corner and a long rambling string of text.

"So, what are we looking at that's so interesting?"

"Loose thread... church reject," she mumbled through a mouthful of gum.

"Church reject? I don't get it."

"We have here a blog post from a very qualified lady, *over*-qual-ified, actually, who volunteered to work for some church group Bunny Jenkins was running to help teenage girls in trouble. The lady says she was not just *dismissed* from both the group and the church, but was also slandered and embarrassed when Gordon and his sister found she was a Native American and a lesbian! The lady, who posted this under the name Beccah, has a Master's de-gree from a university in England and over twenty-five years of teaching experience. She says Gordon called her a 'savage' and a 'blot on the human tribe.'"

"So, this helps us by…."

"Dave, if you can get this woman to testify to what she went through. Or even if you can't, if she'll just tell us what she knows… and I'm sure she knows plenty!"

"So how do we know who she is? Do we have a way to contact her?"

"Of course, you silly old fart! There's a place for comments on her blog space and even an email address to send her messages. All we can do is try. Give me some space to think, Dave. I'll compose a message to her."

I don't know what Yolanda said to the women, but she had a reply within minutes. Beccah had suspected something was very wrong at the Church of the Eternally Blinding Light, but with the half-truths the church was telling, who would ever listen to her. She started her blog page against the church in an attempt to find someone, anyone, who might listen to her side of the story. With something she called 'instant messaging,' Yolanda quickly found out the women's physical address and made an appointment to meet with her face-to-face.

Beccah lived west of Rockport, out past the Bottle Brothel near Copano Bay. Yolanda asked me to take my Saab and drive in circles around Rockport to distract God's Security before she left to keep her appointment with Beccah. She didn't want to be followed, or to compromise Beccah's location.

I led the white car up to Fulton Beach, where I stopped at Rusty's for a beer, then down toward Aransas Pass, where I had another beer at the Handsome Sailor Tiki Bar, then I filled up my tank at a Valero station on the edge of town. On my way back, I stopped at a dollar only store to buy some deodorant and potato chips. God's Security hung on my tail all the way, they stopped where ever I stopped and made a great show of being my shadow. It gave Yolanda plenty of time to get to her meeting and, hopefully, find out what she needed from the church's disgruntled former member.

On arriving back at the office, I flipped my middle finger at God's Security and dragged myself up the office steps to fix myself a drink. I was on my third martini when Yolanda came in.

"Pay dirt, Dave," she sang raising her palm to 'high five' me. "Beccah rocks! She's been gathering information on the church, the Reverend and even his sister. She doesn't have the kind of info we can take to the cops, but she gave me lots of things that can help me, *help us*, gather the gen we need for a bust!"

"How's that?"

"Beccah is in touch with some of the girls who have escaped from Bunny's evil little circle and Arista's Maid Service, as well as some of their other victims. These women are still terrified of Bunny, her minions and the church, but Beccah has them hidden away in a safe house where we can talk to them, where we can get testimony once we have the Reverend and his people in custody."

My lady jumped right back on her computer, researching the group Beccah had worked for. Yolanda found that it was registered as a non-profit under the name Elizabeth Anne Gordon, not Elizabeth or Bunny Jenkins. "Why," Yolanda wondered aloud, "Is it registered under her maiden name? She's been married to the Senator, like, forever!"

I had no quick answer to that.

CHAPTER FIFTEEN

I figured it was time to talk with Saldana again and let him know what we were working on. Although we couldn't disclose who we were talking to, it would be good to let Saldana know we had a few witnesses who could testify down the line.

Saldana had a surprise for me. "I think I found a way to get around local resistance from the cops who have so much loyalty to Gordon and his church. Those documents you gave me? They show a lot of income that can't, technically, be regarded as the church's tax free take. Money from drug dealing or any other illegal activity is *business* income."

"Yeah, as I recall that's how they finally took care of Al Capone." I agreed. "So it should be taxable, but Gordon is running it through the church...."

"That's a criminal act in itself, Holman. But the biggie here is tax evasion, and tax evasion is a federal crime. I remembered an old college friend who's an IRS agent now up in Dallas and he sounds very interested, so I emailed him copies of your photos. I should be hearing back from him soon. I'm pretty sure he'll be sending some federal boys down to ask Gordon a few questions about his, uh, side business."

That would certainly put Gordon a bit off balance. And if he tried to get rid of federal agents, well I kinda liked where this was going.

"So if the Feebs come knocking on Gordon's door, that should get some other people interested. Good thinking, Saldana.

"But the reason I called was to let you know I've found some victims of Gordon's enterprises. When this all goes to trial, they will be happy to help put him and his organization behind bars."

"So when can I get a list of…"

"No list, Saldana! I want to keep them under wraps until you've got these guys in jail."

"Sorry to tell you, Holman. But you should know that within hours of any arrests we make, Gordon and company will be back out on the streets. With the money that church pulls in, you can bet he's lawyered up to his receding hairline. And the first thing he'll do after he makes bail is hire someone to tie up loose ends, like witnesses and accomplices. Your people would be a lot safer if we know who they are and can give them 24-hour protection…"

"I don't think so, Saldana. You've said yourself that there are a lot of police and sheriff's officers who will never believe Gordon is dirty. What's to stop one of Gordon's fans from tying up loose ends before it can get to court? Let's do it my way, okay?"

"Alright, Holman, but you're taking on a big responsibility. You are just one man. You can't offer these folks any real protection."

"I'll hire friends if I have to, Saldana. I'll fly in ex-cops from California if that's what it takes."

The vice cop laughed at this, "It's your case, Holman. Is it worth that much to you? I don't think your client's going to spring for those kinds of expenses."

"Just let me handle it! I'll find a way. And, please, let me know what the feds have to say. I'll be happy to talk with them when they come down."

Saldana laughed at this too. "Don't get your chest too puffed up, Holman. I don't think the FBI or the IRS will want to talk with you. At least not until after they've made their case."

CHAPTER SIXTEEN

After talking to Saldana, I asked Yolanda for Beccah's number and permission to talk with her and warn her of the risks. Yolanda said she'd dial and let me talk to Beccah, the fewer people who knew how to reach her, the better.

Beccah said she was aware of the risks. She was taking special precautions of her own, but at the same time, she told me she would be baiting Gordon to some degree. She just couldn't help herself.

"I've got three or four couples petitioning the church to perform same-sex marriages for them," she said with a smile that came right through the telephone line. "We've threatened to file a class action law suit if he rejects one or all of our requests. He puts up a blustery front, but you can bet we've got him worried! He doesn't need any adverse publicity that could draw attention to his questionable activities."

"That's very brave, Beccah," I told her. "But it's foolish as well. Gordon seems to have a small army of assholes working for him, sadistic little buggers who would probably enjoy hurting you and all your friends. These people are mindless zealots!"

"Hell, Holman," she laughed, "that's half the fun! If we don't stand up for our rights, we'll lose them. I think it was Gandhi that said 'society is only as strong as its weakest member.' I will *not* be that weakest member!"

"I do like your spirit, girl," I told her. "I really hope we'll meet one day soon."

"Oh, I think we will, Holman, I think we will. Can you put Yolanda on the line please?"

I held the phone out and pulled my assistant's attention momentarily away from her computer screen. Yolanda took the instrument and chatted with Beccah for a few minutes. When she hung up, Yolanda wrote something on her legal pad then tore off the page and handed it to me.

"Beccah says you should have all her information. She said you need her address and phone number as well as the address of her safe house and the names of all the women she's protecting. She hopes you'll never have to use this information, but you should have it in case something happens."

"You think I should memorize all this and then eat the paper?" I joked.

Yolanda popped a big bubble gum bubble, making serious eyes at me. "Very droll, Holman, but this is no joking matter. You and I have just taken responsibility for the souls of these women. We must protect them at all cost!" She blew another smaller bubble, then her face softened into a grin. "But why am I telling you this? You're a very enlightened individual, Dave. I sensed that from the first time you came on to me at the India Palace, laying your lame lines on me. That's why I love you!"

It was still light out, but Yolanda had that look in her eye. I followed her back to our crib. She quickly wore this old man out and we fell asleep in each other's arms, a deep dreamless sleep for me.

A commotion outside woke me up. The bedside clock said it

was just after three, dark outside, so it had to be night time. First there was some shouting and a loud scream, that's what had awoken me. Then there was the sound of sirens heading our way from Highway 35. Yolanda grabbed me and clung on. "What was that, Dave? What's going on?"

I pulled on a tee shirt and my cargo shorts then headed down the stairs in my bare feet. I told my girl to wait upstairs in the office.

"Don't come out, no matter what. I'll sort things out. Just wait for me until I give the all clear."

All the lights were on around the corral behind the feed store. Our recued elephant was trumpeting loudly and a man lay quaking in the pen.

Budhan, one of our Indian elephant minders stood over the figure with his arms folded across his chest. The man squirming in the dust was one of my watchers from God's Security Company, not my favorite sadist, but another beer-gutted good ol' boy cast from a similar mold. He was clad in black, including black sneakers and a dark blue ski mask, which Budhan had pulled up to reveal the man's face. I arrived at the corral just as two medics were getting out of an ambulance and heading for the fenced-in pen.

"We have had an intruder, Dave," Budhan announced. "This man entered the pen. I believe he meant to harm our little elephant friend! He has a knife and a gun and a black bag. He also has a dark evil aura. I sensed that he is a very bad man, Dave!"

The two paramedics turned to look at each other. "Someone called 911. Is there an emergency here?" one of them asked.

"Yes, oh yes," Budhan told him. "This man," he lowered his

head toward the moaning figure in the dirt, "he tried to harm our baby elephant. The baby elephant that we just rescued from a rancher who was abusing the poor animal, this man, he tripped in panic and the elephant accidently stepped on him!"

"My god," said the ambulance driver, "that thing must weigh a ton!"

"Not quite a ton," Budhan corrected, but close to that."

I stepped forward. "I don't know if this poor fellow meant to harm the beast," I told them, "but I wish to press charges of trespassing." I picked up the black leather bag the man had dropped. The first thing I recognized was a set of lock picks arranged in a clear plastic case. There was also a pair of purple latex gloves. "Whatever he was doing, this man had no good business on my property at this time of night."

A Rockport police car had entered the property at some time during our conversation. The policeman took up a position at my side.

"Trespassing charges," he echoed. "You're Dave Holman?"

I told him I was and asked if he'd like to see some ID.

"No sir," he told me. "The chief has mentioned you a few times. He likes you and says he's glad you're here helping to keep order. We'll take this man into custody. You can come down tomorrow morning and fill out a complaint."

"I think we should add attempted burglary to that complaint," I said handing the lawman the lock picks and gloves from the bag.

After the cops had left and the ambulance had taken the God's Security man to the hospital in Corpus, I spoke with Budhan.

"The man was about to climb up the stairs to where you and Miss Yolanda sleep," he told me. "I could feel that he meant you harm. Just before he reached bottom step with his rope and black bag, I awakened Krishna, our little elephant. I told her to attack the man. The man, he panicked and made threatening gestures at Krishna. Naturally, she ran forward, right over his body!"

"But the man was found in her pen…"

"Yes, I dragged his body there while he was passed out, before I called 911 on my cell phone. I also buried his rope in the big pile of pellets we use to cover the smell of elephant poop. I will dispose of it tomorrow!"

I praised Budhan for his quick thinking, adding that it might be good to keep the rope as more evidence. I could tell the police I found it when daylight exposed a larger area of the property.

When Budhan returned to his small tent, I ventured forth with my flashlight and located the God's Security car. It was half a mile down Market Street, with the keys in the ignition. The interior light had been set so that it didn't come on when I opened the door. There was no one around at this hour, now just short of four, so I got in and started the engine. I drove up Broadway along Little Bay toward Fulton. Just short of the Lighthouse Inn, I make a sharp right turn, aiming the vehicle toward the water. There was a pile of old, worn concrete blocks on the narrow beach and I picked one up. I undid my seatbelt and wiped the steering wheel, keys and door handle with my pocket handkerchief. Then I placed a large breeze-block on the accelerator and put the car in drive as I bailed. From the lawn of the Fulton Mansion, just across the road, I watched as the big white car chugged into the waves, hesitated, and then slid forward and under the green gulf water.

I whistled a happy tune as I walked home. What the hell, I could use the exercise. Back in the office I took out the bottom drawer of the filing cabinet. From under the drawer, I retrieved an old Walther P-38 automatic. It was a souvenir my father had brought back from World War II. Stamped into the dark blue finish of the slide, there was a small German eagle holding a swastika. I brought the gun to my desk, took out a rag and some oil. I unloaded the gun, dismantled it and cleaned all its parts thoroughly before reassembling the weapon, pushing a full clip of nines into the gun's butt and working the slide to put one in the chamber. I left the gun in the bottom desk drawer, behind the office bottle, where I could reach it quick and easy. I was back in bed, snuggled against Yolanda before the sun came up. When her eyes gave me a questioning look, I told her, "You really don't want to know."

CHAPTER SEVENTEEN

I awoke to full bright sun through the window and someone shouting as they pounded on the office door. Yolanda shook sleep from her eyes and gave me a questioning look. I pulled on my shorts and shirt from the night before and went through to open the office door.

Reverend Clemson Gordon stood on the mat outside the portal to my inner sanctum. He was bright red, breathing heavily, his eyes watered and there was a trickle of snot below his nose.

"God damn it, Holman... as the Lord is my witness I'm gonna kill you!"

I gave him a disdainful look, stood back from the entranceway and motioned to my plastic visitor's chair. The man took three steps forward and fell back into the green plastic, his breath still ragged and his eyes rolling heavenward. For a moment or two I thought he might be having a heart attack, then I thought "this is one man I do *not* want to give the kiss of life!"

Gordon's eyes slowly came back down to focus on me. He took a series of long deep breaths then rolled his head around on his neck, first one direction and then the other.

"Holman, you really piss me off!" he said loudly, but in a calmer voice. "You nearly killed one of my employees. You sicced your God damn elephant on him. He's in the hospital with three cracked ribs and a collapsed lung!"

The preacher man took another deep breath. "Then you somehow pushed valuable church property out into the Gulf of Mexico!" I got a call first thing this morning from some towing company that the Fulton Chief of Police had them pull one of my security vehicles out of the water and I have to pick up the cost of retrieval and storage for the damn thing! Do you know what they're charging me for rescuing that damn truck? They claim they had to hire a driver to swim out there with the tow chain!"

I remained silent, letting him wind down before I entered the conversation. When his appearance became more relaxed and normal, I said," Your employee was in the act of burglarizing my office when he must have tripped into the elephant's pen. And you vehicle, with your own churches security logo on the door was being used in that criminal enterprise. I guess your boy couldn't see it was an animal pen sneaking around my property in the dark..."

"Damn it, Holman, you'll pay for this..."

"Perhaps we should move this little chat to one of the interview rooms at the Rockport Police station, Reverend? I'm heading there anyway to file a complaint against your dumb lackey."

The man's face was starting to bloom with bright crimson again, "Holman, I'm warning you!" He started to get out of his chair, reaching his hands across my desk and toward my throat. I ducked and grabbed the Walther from my desk drawer. As I stood up myself, I shoved the gun barrel deep into his flabby midriff causing the man to cough and choke.

"You know you're the one on the wrong side of the law here, Gordon," I told him. "You're lackey got himself hurt trying to commit a crime. He used one of your church vehicles in attempting to commit that crime. The Rockport cops have his little bag of tricks in evidence. That would be the bag with his gloves, lock jimmying equipment, a few yards of rope and more. I think I'm the one on the moral high ground here, *Reverend*!" I sneered the last word to show I had no respect for his high title.

"And another thing, if you don't want me to make a big media circus out of the actions of you and your boy, you'll pull back your security people and stop trying to intimidate me by following everywhere I go. Do we understand each other in this, *Reverend*?"

Clemson Gordon dropped back heavily into his seat again looking defeated. He leaned his head back and spoke toward the ceiling, "Alright, Holman, you win this round…. But the war isn't over yet! You quit following my sister around and nosing into my business! You understand me?"

"I stopped following your sister over a week ago."

"Well call off whoever is workin' for you then."

"Gordon, I don't *have* anyone working for me, and I don't have anyone following your sister. I learned what I needed to know early on."

Gordon cast suspicious eyes on me. He slowly came out of his chair and backed towards the door to my office. I kept the ancient automatic pointed his direction and followed him out. I walked behind him down the hall to the stairs and clocked his journey to his car. When he'd fired up the big gray Cadillac he was driving and turned out onto Market Street, I lowered the gun and returned to the office.

CHAPTER EIGHTEEN

Yolanda came out of our apartment after Clem Gordon was gone. She was dressed casually in what I believe are called peddle-pushers, white pants that came down to mid calf, and a colorful blouse decorated with scenes of Los Angeles locations. I recognized the Santa Monica Pier and the street sign for Rodeo Drive. It had some black fringe along the bottom.

"Coffee, Dave?"

"Yeah, I could really use a cup or three. What a way to start the day… looking into Gordon's ugly mug!"

Outside I heard some commotion. Afraid that the right Reverend or some of his minions might have returned, I rushed out and down following the sounds. What I found was Budhan, Payush and Darpaknu gathered around the baby elephant. They had another rental truck backed up to the corral entrance and were coaxing the small pachyderm up the ramp of the medium-sized stake truck.

"Krishna is strong enough now for the journey to Tennessee," Darpaknu said with a broad smile. "She showed that her spirit is back when she defended your home last night."

"Also," Budhan added, "we are afraid that these bad men you are dealing with might misplace their anger at you on poor little Krishna. They might return and try to hurt our baby."

"So we feel it is safer if we move her now," added Darpaknu. "We are entrusted with her safety. It is a responsibility we do not take lightly!"

Yolanda walked up beside me and nodded a greeting to the men. She touched my arm and gave me a kiss, then went over to stroke the pachyderm's trunk, laying her forehead on the elephant's. When she had said her goodbye to the beast, she hugged each of her helpers in turn and wished them a safe journey.

Back upstairs, my lady sliced a couple of bagels and put them in the toaster, then turned to the espresso machine. I went to the fridge and found some cream cheese and lox.

"Could you slice up a little red onion while you're at it?" she asked.

I grabbed a fresh onion from the fruit bowl on the counter. "So do I need to bring you up to speed about last night?"

"I talked to Budhan this morning after the cops left," she told me filling our cups with hot liquid and sampling her own, "so I've got a pretty good idea. What was that about Gordon's car? There was something said about it being towed out of some water?"

"Yeah, childish of me, I guess." I gave her my brightest and best little boy grin. "I just couldn't resist driving his security car into Aransas Bay. I honestly didn't think it was that deep, but she disappeared briefly, then came floating up and rolled over. I'm surprised it was spotted so quickly. Probably a little treat for one of the shrimp boat captains making an early run...."

Yolanda laughed so hard she sprayed coffee from her nose and mouth onto the table. That started me laughing as well. I could tell this was going to be a good day!

CHAPTER NINETEEN

After my visit to the Rockport Police station where I filed trespassing, assault and attempted burglary charges against my previous night's intruder, I spent the morning getting caught up on paperwork while Yolanda surfed the Internet for more information about Gordon's church. Around two, we went up to Rusty's for a drink and a late lunch. Halfway through our baskets of fried crawfish tails and fried Jalapeño peppers, Yolanda's phone rang. She answered, listened for a few beats and then her face lit up.

"Beccah, that sounds like fun! ...What time do they usually arrive? ...And is there a safe place to park? ...Yes, of course. I'll pick you up around seven."

"Okay," I told her, "I get that you were talking to Beccah. So what was that all about?"

"Beccah has a plan," Yolanda grinned at me. "She says the maids will be cleaning Gordon's big house on Mustang Island tonight, she just talked to one of the girls she is trying to help to escape from the cleaning service. Gordon is supposed to be at a board meeting or something at the church, so it will only be a few security guards there, and the security people try to avoid anything to do with the maids. They look down on them as poor brown people."

"So you're planning to help Beccah get this girl out of there?"

"Better than that, Dave, we plan to do a little spying. Beccah and I will have a nice look around the place. Gordon may have more evidence hidden in an office at home, maybe things too terrible to leave in the church office!"

"That place is supposed to be heavily guarded. Are you planning to somehow hijack the Arista's van to get through the gate?"

"It should be easier than that, Dave. Beccah say she knows a path through the dunes from the beach. When there are late meetings at the church, some of the guards from the house are sent to the church along with Gordon for extra protection, which means there will only be one man patrolling the dunes according to some of Beccah's girls who have worked there. We can easily get by him."

"I don't know, Yo, this sounds very dangerous to me."

"Dave, I am a big girl, and Beccah is a big girl too! We can take care of ourselves. And maybe we'll also find some interesting things for the Senator as well, or for the police."

CHAPTER TWENTY

O f course another trip to Castaways was required to create good maid disguises, but we arrived there to find that the thrift shop was closed. We never thought that a volunteer run business would close at three in the afternoon, but that's what their sign said they did, everyday.

Another call to Beccah helped us to re-group. Beccah told Yolanda she had plenty of worn old clothes in a rag bag that had come from girls she had rescued. She always saw to it that her rescues got fresh clothes before they went to the safe house. Yolanda dropped me back at the office and continued on to Beccah's place to go through the collection of rags and see what might fit her willowy frame.

My lady returned with a sorry outfit of torn red jeans, bling-covered sandals and a baggy A&M tee shirt. She tore up one of her old blouses to create a passable head scarf. "You'd blend in at any homeless shelter in the land," I told her, eliciting a broad smile. "You ready for a drink?"

"No, Dave," she said with a disappointed look. "For this one, I think I'd better keep all my wits about me,"

As Yolanda relayed it to me the next morning over breakfast, she and Beccah had driven down the sand from one of the Port Aransas beach access roads to the mile marker just short of Gordon's compound. They left the Thing parked in a sheltered ravine among the dunes where it couldn't be seen from the compound's security post at the top of the grassy hillocks. Halfway up the rise of sand, they discovered that there was more than one lone rent-a-cop on dune duty, but they managed to elude the men on patrol.

"That should have alerted us that something wasn't quite right," she told me, "but we didn't think too much about it. Maybe some of the guys just liked to hang around with their buddies when they weren't on duty. That was my reasoning, anyway.

"Then, when we crawled out of the brush, we noticed that Clem Gordon's gray Cadillac was still parked outside the big house in the center of the compound. We figured maybe he was running late and hadn't left for his meeting yet. When Arista's van arrived and the car was still there, we started to have some real concerns, but we snuck around the van anyway and fell in with the maids when they piled out and lined up. In for a penny, in for a pound, we figured."

"Yo," I asked her, "what were you really thinking? Where was your head at?"

"Come one, Dave," she replied. "We were on a mission. Like, licensed to kill and all that stuff!

"Yo, you are *not* James Bond... not even a *female* James Bond..."

She gave me an evil wink. "Well, I'm here telling you all this, am I not?"

"Okay, alright, so what happened next?" I was getting caught up in the story. I couldn't help myself.

"Beccah and I got sent up to the top floor to clean. On the way up the stairs, Beccah was able to speak with the young girl she was hoping to rescue, who had also been assigned the top floor, though not the end of the passageway where we were to work. The space we were to clean was west of the stairs, where the Reverend's private master suite was located.

"Approaching the door to Clem Gordon's private lair, we could hear the loud sounds of unrestrained sex, heavy breathing and moaning. Reverend Gordon was loudly taking his lord's name in vain as his breathing approached a climax. Beccah and I looked back at the young girl who had accompanied us up to the top floor. We motioned her to come to us and asked her what was going on.

"It is Mr. Gordon and his wife," the girl told us, "We must wait until he opens the bedroom door to let us know they will be showering before we go in there to strip the sheets from their bed and empty the waste baskets. We bring the sheets down to Mona, who does the laundry and put fresh ones on the bed quickly, before they come out of the bathroom, then we come back and clean the bathroom just before we leave the property. They should be asleep by then. Even if they are not, we avert our eyes and they ignore us."

"You said Gordon and his wife?" Yolanda had asked.

"Yes, they are very passionate, and very kinky too, is that the word? They do strange things together, and sometimes he ties her like a slave and parades her through the house for all the staff to see that he is her master! This does not seem right, but then he is very rich, so...."

"Wait a minute," Beccah had said. "Reverend Gordon is not married! So who is this woman that is pretending to be his wife?"

"Oh, it is his wife," the young lady assured us. "She is Elizabeth Anne Gordon! Elizabeth Anne is what he always calls her. She lives here with him!"

"So Gordon is having it off with his sister," I said, interrupting Yolanda's tale.

"It would seem so," Yolanda told me. "But at that point, I was near panic. If Gordon should open the door, he would surely recognize me and call the guards. I told Beccah we had to get out, right away!

"So Beccah doubled over and started moaning like she was sick. I told the other girl we had to help her. We were almost to the stairs when I heard the door opening behind us and Gordon asking what was wrong. In my best Mexican accent I shouted that the girl was sick and we were taking her outside to throw up so she wouldn't soil his pretty carpet. I said it in a concerned voice without turning my head around. As we started down the stairs I could hear Gordon shout, 'damn Mexicans! They'll do anything to get out of a little work. You bitches better hurry back up here and get some fresh linen on my bed or I'll see that you... all three of you, get a good beating!'

"There was no one in the entryway between the stairway and the front door, so Beccah and I stripped off our maid outfits and tossed them behind one of the couches. Beccah had brought some large black trash bags, one with arm holes and a head hole cut in the bottom. We slipped the cut bag over the young girl's head and wrapped the others around her waist and legs, then we ran in a crouch for the dunes. We crawled on our bellies like snakes through the sand and scrub. The guards were easy to spot, as they were smoking. We avoided the red glow of their cigarettes above the tall grasses while we circled past their sentry patrol walkway. The girl with us was terrified, but Beccah told the woman that she was using her Native American magic to make us invisible. We stayed in the tall grass and sea grape all way to the ravine where the Thing was. When I got the car started, we drove slowly back up the beach without turning on the lights. I avoided using the brakes as I was afraid the sudden flare of our tail lights might give us away."

"That's some story," I told her. "But I would think a sick girl and two others not returning to their appointed jobs must have alerted Gordon that something was wrong. The overseer from Arista's would confirm that at least one employee was missing."

"Our little rescue girl, Danielle, told us that Gordon would probably just assume everyone was too afraid of him and his men to do anything wrong. He would continue with his evening, taking a long shower with his 'wife' and he wouldn't notice anything was wrong until they emerged from the bath to find the bed sheets had not been changed. He would then most likely call one of the security men and have them send another maid up to make his bed quickly and then tell them to check on the whereabouts of the first set of cleaners, ordering his guards to punish them severely when they were located."

"But by now, I'm sure he knows something was going on there." I reminded her, "He's got to be mad as hell, and he probably suspects you and I are a part of it."

"Beccah says girls do sometimes disappear from Arista's service. She says she even suspects that the security people have, on occasion, grabbed a girl or two, raped and killed them and buried their bodies under the sand dunes. If they're on Gordon's property, no one else is likely to discover their graves."

CHAPTER TWENTY ONE

Clemson Gordon's call came around three-thirty in the afternoon, but I soon learned that his call had nothing to do with missing maids or strangers trespassing on his property.

"The gloves are coming off, Holman! You've gone too far this time! I've got an office full of government men here going through my church records. They're telling me they intend to seize my church financial books, that they received a tip along with evidence that I owe them income tax because all my business ain't church business.

"I know this has to be your doin', Holman. My security team saw someone sneakin' around my grounds and maybe even comin' out of my office a little over a week ago. I know it was you, Holman. It had to have been you!"

I gave him a hollow laugh. "Gordon, it sounds to me like you might have gotten up any number of noses in the area. You've been railing on about homosexuals, non-whites, non-believers and who knows who else. You've come out against women's rights, abortion, illegals... Any number of people might be working to bring you down."

"Sure, Holman, but I still think it's you. I think you're orchestrating this. You strike me as the kind of liberal do-gooder who would know all these people that the Bible has condemned and you're the kind of white knight fool to try and help them bring down America's Christians! You're an evil man, Holman!"

"One might say the same of you, Gordon! Just what is this business of yours that the IRS is asking about?"

I heard coughing, choking and some heavy breathing just before the line went dead.

CHAPTER TWENTY TWO

A small storm front suddenly burst on the scene from out in the gulf in the late afternoon. The sky was getting darker by the minute and spectacular electrical fireworks were lighting up the sky as pouring rain moved west from the barrier islands. Of course we needed the rain, south Texas always needs rain, but the timing struck me as less than helpful.

Around six Ken Millar called to tell me Gordon had been arrested by the feds, but had already made bail and a light bail at that. The judge was a member of Gordon's church and, while he understood the seriousness of the charges, felt that Clem Gordon could be trusted to make his court appearance next week, so he had set bail at fifty-thousand. The FBI had first asked that bail be denied, then suggested something around two million dollars.

Later, as Yolanda and I were watching an old movie, the phone rang again. "Tell the Senator that his wife isn't going to cause him any more problems in this election." Clem Gordon's voice had a cold and hollow note to it. "He can campaign without any worry that her, ah, activities will hurt his chances."

"Why don't you call him yourself, Gordon?"

"I just did, Mr. Holman. He was downright rude to me. I asked him to pull a few simple strings for me... to, you know, maybe get some of the federal heat off my back. Burt Jenkins told me it was far beyond his capabilities, that I should call my U.S. Senator or someone else in Washington. And after all I've done for him over the years! Don't you think that's kinda small minded, Mr. Holman?"

I started to reply, but the man cut me off. With an evil laugh he shouted, "Fuck you, Mr. Holman... And fuck my brother-in-law the righteous Texas Senator!" His laugh turned into something out of an old horror film, loud and echoing off stone castle walls. I pressed down the button to cut him off then dialed Senator Jenkins.

"Good evening, Senator," I began.

"Is that you, Holman?" his voice projected stressful tension. "Do you know where Bunny is?"

"No, Senator, I don't know the whereabouts of your wife. I rang you because I just had a strange call from your brother-in-law. I don't know if you're aware, but he was arrested today for income tax fraud. He said to tell you that your wife wasn't going to be a problem for you in getting re-elected. What does that mean and why call me?"

"Bunny isn't here, Holman. We were supposed to meet at Latitude 28°02′ for dinner, but she didn't show. And her cell phone has been going straight to voice mail all evening. I'm very concerned, Holman. This isn't like her. I mean, she is out on her own a lot of the time and we don't talk that much, but when she says we'll get together, she never stands me up without some kind of word! I'm thinkin' something must have happened to her."

"Calm down, Senator," I told him. "Why don't you call the police? Maybe she had car trouble or an accident. I'm sure she's okay. If she's been admitted to a hospital, they might be trying to call you right now."

"I don't know, Holman, I've got a sick feeling about this. Isn't there anything you can do to help?"

"I can't do anything more than what you can do yourself. I wouldn't know where to start looking. You know her habits and haunts. I think you need to call around. If she's still missing in the morning, we can get together and I'll set out a plan to search for her. If she shows up, call and let me know, doesn't matter what time it is, okay?"

"Well..."

"Give the local state trooper barracks a call, Senator. And call some of her friends. I'm sure she'll turn up!"

Another hour into the night and the phone rang again, this time it was Beccah. Danielle, the girl she and Yolanda had rescued, had received a terrified call from one of the other girls. Danielle had given the girl Beccah's number in hopes that her friend might be helped to escape from Arista's bondage as well.

The girl told Danielle that she'd heard an awful fight between the Reverend and his wife. Elizabeth Anne had been shouting, then screaming and begging for her life. A short while later, two of the security men had carried a long tube of rolled-up rug from the Reverend's bedroom, down the stairs and shoved it into the trunk of the man's big gray Cadillac. When they'd gone into the master suite to change the linen, there was much blood on the sheets and more blood on the floor and walls. No one had seen Elizabeth Anne leave the compound.

"I thought you should know about this, Holman," Beccah said. "I don't know how credible this woman is, but there might be something to it. Just in case, maybe you should give the police a call, have them pay a little courtesy call on Gordon just to check things out."

I told her that was good thinking. When we'd rung off, I called a man I knew with the Port Aransas department. We chatted for a minute about the storm outside, how spectacular the lightning was out over the Gulf and that much of Mustang Island had lost power before I made my request.

I knew that here in Rockport we were under a tornado advisory, and told him I knew it was a lot to ask on such a night. He promised me that he'd stop by Gordon's compound when he got a break and take a look then give me a call back.

It was well past midnight when I heard back from my Port Aransas cop friend.

"The security man on the gate welcomed me in. That in itself seemed a little suspicious. Usually they don't want us around the place, except for a couple of the guys who moonlight there with that God's Security outfit. The place was all lit up with emergency generators, but the Rev's bedroom appeared to be squeaky clean, no blood anywhere that we could see. Gordon wasn't around, nor was the sister. The gate guard claimed no one had seen Gordon all day. He denied that Gordon's car had been there that evening and told me that he believed Reverend Gordon had gone out of town for a few days on business. One of the maids who was getting into the cleaning company van to leave appeared to have a bloody nose and a shiner, but the guy who brings them around each night told me the girl had tripped and fell. The girl nodded her head that it was true, so we couldn't say much. All the maids looked terrified and claimed they didn't understand our questions as they only spoke Spanish.

I thanked the man for checking the situation out for me but he laughed and said it was such a weird night anyway that it was nice to have something to do beside rescue stranded motorists from the flooded streets.

I thought about calling Saldana, but decided it could wait until morning. Yolanda was already asleep and I could use a little rest myself if I could fall asleep with the earth-shaking rumble of thunder all around.

CHAPTER TWENTY THREE

Yolanda has a tiny television with a four or five inch screen that she watches in the bathroom sometimes while she's dressing or putting on makeup. She had it on this morning to check on a small storm that had passed through overnight. There had been a lot of lightning and any number of tornado warnings. I could hear that she'd turned up the volume then, moments later, she called my name.

"Dave? You'd better get in here and see this, Dave! Some early morning beach walkers found a body near the Port A jetty, Bunny Jenkins's body they're saying."

I rushed into the small room. On the miniature screen, a thin bottle blond holding a microphone stood on the beach, her face bathed in flashing blue and red lights. There was an ambulance and two police cars behind her and a large, colorful beach towel that appeared to be partially covering a body.

"… the Port Aransas police chief, who is a close friend of Senator Jenkins has positively identified the body which washed up on Magee County Beach this morning as the Senator's wife, Bunny Jenkins. The body appears to be badly battered from storm waves throwing it against the jetty for much of the night. It was reported that Mrs. Jenkins had gone sailing yesterday, before the storm with fellow parishioners of her church. Just after the storm began, the local Coast Guard station received a radio message that Mrs. Jenkins had fallen overboard and was missing. Local officers are saying that they believe this is a death by misadventure. This is Tina Perez, Channel 12 News.

I rang the Senator immediately. His line was answered by one of his aides. "The Senator has been informed of his wife's unfortunate accident," the woman told me. "He has been given a sedative and said he doesn't want to talk to anyone right now."

Next I placed a call to Lieutenant Saldana. I told him about the call from one of the maids telling about the fight and blood, then I told him that Officer Daley of the Port A cops had gone to the Gordon compound, but had found no evidence of foul play.

"I don't believe this was an accident," Saldana firmly stated. "I've requested that Bunny Jenkins' body be sent here to Corpus Christi for an autopsy. The Senator has given his permission for the move as next of kin."

"What do you expect to find?"

"I'm not sure just yet, but if it was murder, there will be some clue. I was suspicious right away when I heard that her body had been slammed against the rocks off the jetty all night. A chief I know at the Coast Guard station said the captain of the boat Bunny supposedly had been swept from by a wave had sailed from one of the marinas on North Padre early yesterday afternoon. When he'd radioed his mayday call, the man had given his position as somewhere just north of the state park. I know storm surf can be erratic, but I don't think it would be enough to carry a body eight or nine miles north."

"I would agree with you on that, Saldana. Hitting those rocks a few times would also cover up marks from a human inflicted beating. Also, Bunny was supposed to meet the Senator at a restaurant in Rockport last night for dinner. If she was planning to be in Rockport by eight or nine to eat, it doesn't seem logical that she would go out sailing just a few hours before. Where was Clem Gordon last night, do we know?"

"Now that's another curious matter, Holman. No one has seen the Right Reverend since shortly after he made bail yesterday. He's not at his home and no one has seen him around his church, at least that's what they're saying."

"Has anyone questioned his bail bondsman?"

"Yeah, the man who is guaranteeing his bond told us the Reverend promised he would stay at his compound on Mustang Island. He'd be there if there were any questions."

"But he's not there… has anyone been to his place to look for him?" This story was beginning to pique my curiosity.

"When we couldn't locate him this morning to inform him of his sister's death, the FBI sent a team over there to tear the place apart. They ended up taking a couple of the compounds' security people into custody for running interference. Those God squaders kept getting in their faces, almost like they were trying to buy time while Gordon was on the move through the place. I've sent a crime scene team of my own over there as well to tear apart Gordon's bedroom. If there are any traces of blood to be found, we'll find them. The most thorough cleaning in the world can't wipe out all the traces!"

"Curiouser and curiouser," I mumbled. "If these maids heard a fight, possibly a murder sometime after dark, but the Senator's wife was supposed to already be out sailing, this would have to be well thought out, like pre-meditated murder!"

"It would certainly look that way to me. I'll give you a call when they finish the autopsy," he promised.

I shared Saldana's and my conversation with Yolanda. "You still have your gun handy?" she asked with fearful eyes. "If that nasty minister man can't be found, and we know he is very mad at you, he may be on his way here to kill you."

I tsk tsked her, but Yolanda did have a valid point.

"Just be calm," I told her. "I can take care of myself. And I'll be here to protect you as well."

After I said it, I started going through my desk. There was a holster in there somewhere that had come back from Germany with the gun all those years ago. It had a small sleeve on the outside that held an extra clip of ammo for the gun. I never liked the holster, however, as it had a German eagle and swastika burned into the leather on the outside for all the world to see. I took off my belt and threaded it through the loops on the holster before strapping it back on my jeans.

Yolanda gave me a telling look. "Yes, Mr. Big Guy who can take care of himself. I thought you might see it my way."

I took the P-38 out of my desk drawer and slipped it into the holster. "I've got another gun around here somewhere," I told my lady. "Do you want to carry one as well?"

"Oh, no, Dave, I do not like guns! I have my martial arts training. And I can run fast, too!

"I hope that will be enough. You know I don't like violence…."

CHAPTER TWENTY FOUR

I moved Yolanda's tiny television out to my desk. I didn't own an idiot box myself as I had no use for the drivel that usually came from it, but today was a different situation. There was a crazy man, possibly a killer out there on the loose, a man who had a special grudge against me.

We left the small set on and watched the news updates throughout the morning. Everyone was looking for Gordon. The feds suspected that he was fleeing from their list of charges against him, the Corpus Christi Police and the Nueces County Sheriffs badly wanted to talk to Gordon and a few state troopers had questions as well.

Saldana called just after lunch. "Because the woman is a state Senator's wife," he told me, "her autopsy jumped to the head of the list and was completed as soon as possible. We had the coroner's people work right through their midday meal time to get the job done. The doctor's first discovery was that Elizabeth Anne had a broken hyoid bone, just as I had predicted. That proves that the woman was strangled. From the amount of blood she had lost, the doctor postulated that most of her cuts, bruises and abrasions had occurred *before* she was choked to death." Saldana took a deep breath. A moment of quiet told me he was scanning a report or list of facts or something, then he continued. "The majority of her injuries had nothing to do with being thrown against the Port Aransas jetty or any other rocks.

"The coroner's finding further indicates that, for what it's worth, Elizabeth Anne Jenkins was dead for a while before she went overboard. She had no seawater in her lungs." I told him I was not surprised by any of this.

"I sent out men to bring Gordon in for questioning right after we talked this morning," Saldana told me. "But Gordon can't be found. He seems to have vanished from the face of the earth!"

"Do you think he might have fled to Mexico," I asked. "He likely has a few associates there who could hide him for awhile."

"I think that, with the FBI on his tail, his cartel type buddies won't want much more to do with him. The south of the border crowd probably already has his face on a target. Besides, Gordon thrives on celebrity... and he doesn't like common brown types. I don't believe he'll head for the border."

Saldana ended the call and I went back to watching television. A bulletin told us that one of the God's Security men the feds had arrested that morning for obstructing officers had been shot in a daring attempt to escape from custody. He had been hospital-ized with a bullet in his thigh. The man was conscious, but wasn't talking to anyone.

Saldana called again and asked if I could come down to Corpus headquarters and talk with him. "I think we should brain storm this together, Holman. You can think a little outside the 'Texas cop' box and maybe jar some new ideas loose on all this. Also," he chuckled, "you could share some of those 'big city' California cop ideas we locals usually don't want to hear about."

"Keep the door locked and don't go anywhere," I warned Yolanda. "I'm sure Gordon has more to worry about right now than revenge."

"If you say so, Dave, you be careful too!" she put her arms around my neck giving me a deep, long kiss and a tight hug.

I was quickly waved through by the front desk at the main Corpus police center and given a uniformed escort. Saldana had a corner office on the second floor looking out toward the Lawrence Street T-Head and the yacht harbor. He stood and stepped out from behind his desk to shake my hand as I was escorted into the room.

"Let's go over to one of the conference rooms," he said. "I've got a few other people I want you to meet." We walked out through the vice squad bullpen and down a short hall to a windowless room with a long table and eight swivel chairs. There was already a tray of doughnuts and a couple carafes of coffee waiting. "We're going to make this our ops room for the case for the time being."

Ken Millar was hanging there as well along with two other plain clothes men whom I didn't recognize. Ken made introductions.

Jeff Blakely was a street cop with vice and Jerry Sanchez a sergeant in homicide. We all shook hands while my young uniformed escort poured us coffee and set some paper plates on the table.

"Overnight we rounded up a number of so-called church elders who were dealing in narcotics and methamphetamines," Blakely told me. "The church attorneys who came for Gordon don't seem so interested in these hoods."

"Hopefully they'll panic and roll over on some of their buddies," Millar added.

"Your assistant recognizing those codes on the church rooster was a big help, Holman," Blakely directed at me sincerely. "We would have caught it eventually, but she saved us valuable time. Tell her thanks from us."

"I'm hoping we can get more good leads from some of our own men who attend Gordon's church. Could you send in Dixon and Smythe please, John?" Millar asked the young man. My blue suited guide saluted and left the office. A minute later two other uniformed cops entered, one of them with a cocky walk and a smirk on his face. "Wipe that look off your face, Smythe," Millar frowned. "This is serious business. Clemson Gordon is missing and he needs to be found. We could use a little cooperation here!"

"*You're* trying to frame the Reverend and discredit his ministry," Smythe replied in a smart aleck tone of voice. "What ever happened to freedom of religion in this country," he sneered, adding a delayed, "*sir!*"

"You want a few weeks time off without pay?" Saldana offered, rising up from his seat. Smythe stood up a little straighter and lost his cocky look. "No sir. I, I've got a family to feed sir."

"Then leave your personal beliefs and feelings outside the door and give us some answers here. Reverend Gordon hasn't been tried yet or found guilty of anything, but we need to locate him for questioning. He's definitely a person-of-interest in some things this department is looking into and possibly a murder suspect as well. We want to talk to you and Dixon here because you go to the man's church and maybe you can help us locate him. And if he is innocent, maybe you'll have the chance to stand up for the man and help prove his innocence."

Millar added, "Do you have any idea where Reverend Gordon might be, ah, staying? The sooner we find him and talk to him, the sooner we can put all this behind us."

With a worried look, Dixon joined the conversation. "Ah, sir? You do know about Reverend Gordon's hurricane house, don't you?"

"Hurricane house?" I asked.

Dixon gave me a "who's this" look but went on to explain. "You know, a safe place a few miles inland where folks can evacuate to when there's a big storm heading toward the coast."

"Gordon has a hurricane house?" Millar asked. "Where might that be?"

"I think it's in Cuero," Smythe put in. "You know, out to the west of Goliad?"

Saldana called the uniform who'd served us the coffee back in from his post by the door. "Can you give a call to the Cuero Police, John? Ask them to check around and find out if Clemson Gordon owns a house in their city." The man saluted with a crisp, "Yes sir!" and left the room again.

As John was leaving, another officer came in with a small package. "Saldana? Someone just left a DVD at the front desk for you." He handed the slim, black plastic case to the senior vice cop. "The FedEx guy told the desk sergeant the package was dropped off at one of those mail centers out on South Padre Island Drive. I unwrapped it, put the envelope in an evidence bag and sent it straight to the lab."

"We better get a monitor and a video player in here," Millar told the man. "Smythe? Dixon? We will need to talk to you further, but for now I'm going to ask you both to wait out in the squad room."

The two young uniforms left along with John and the messenger who had brought the disc. The messenger and John returned, pushing in a tall mobile cart with a large flat panel TV and a DVD player. The set was quickly plugged in, the disc inserted and the room lights were dimmed.

CHAPTER TWENTY FIVE

T he video was in color, the images sharp and easily recognizable. Gordon was standing behind the pulpit of his church. On the screen, there was a television sitting on a tall table behind the Reverend. On the small screen in the picture, Channel Three's local morning news and talk program was running with the sound turned off. Whoever had filmed this wanted to be sure it was understood that the video was current, only a few hours old. All the details of the church altar were there and easily recognizable.

Then on the video Clemson Gordon cleared his throat and began speaking. "It brings me great displeasure to learn that so many of the people of Texas have turned against me... have turned against Jesus and against the One True Church. This is a sad day for Christians, and for Christianity. But I will not stand for this blasphemy, and I will *not* take this laying down."

The Reverend's eyes burned with a mad, crazy fire. He was shouting, and had small foamy bits of spittle around the corners of his mouth. "Whether you believe it or not, God is on my side! I am on the righteous path and I will not be stopped or brought down by a bunch of Keystone Cops!

"Detective Saldana, Agents Beckworth and Hobson of the IRS, whoever those FBI assholes are, keyhole peeper Holman... and any other of you liberal, bleeding heart atheist bastards out there who are trying to stand in my way... I will kill you! Each and every one of you! I promise I will kill you! Just like when I arranged that accident for your meddling chief of police! I swear this on the church in which I stand!" The man then broke into a fit of crazed laughter and the screen went blank.

Saldana was on his feet even before the disc ended. "John, have my men send a SWAT team over to the church right away! If there's even a chance the man might be there, we need to go to that church and look around… look into anywhere a man might hide."

We sat mostly in silence for half an hour, made some small talk, ate doughnuts and drank coffee. Finally the telephone on a side table rang. Millar grabbed it before the first ring finished.

"Millar here, what have you got?"

His face went from stoic to disappointed very quickly. He said, "Thank you," then placed the instrument back in its cradle.

"I've had a contingent of men guarding the church," he told us. "Sergeant Mendoza was, and still is in charge. My first thought when I looked at that video was that Gordon might have burst in there with his security people and taken out our men, but that doesn't seem to be the case.

"Mendoza says they've been there all day. A pair of officers has been stationed in the main sanctuary right near the altar at all times, and there hasn't been any sign of Gordon or his people. They haven't seen anyone with video cameras there either. I don't know how he could have faked that video, but somehow, he must have!"

John, the young uniform who was acting as Saldana's helper piped up. "Sir, I overheard Smythe and Dixon out in the hall. You might want to bring them in and ask…."

"Okay, send them in John. Maybe if they see the video, it will jog their memories a bit."

Dixon and Smythe remained standing as the DVD was re-played for their benefit. When it was over, Saldana asked the men, "Any idea where this video could have been shot?"

Dixon looked at his partner, as if seeking permission to speak. When Smythe wouldn't look him in the eye, he laughed and said, "Reverend Gordon has stage sets designed to look like his church in a number of places. He has one in his place on Mustang Island and another at the hurricane house. He may even have one at the retreat in the Rio Grande Valley, for all I know. The studios are part of the church's cable television network. The church broadcasts inspirational messages twenty-four hours a day, along with a daily gospel hour featuring the church choir and daily Bible study."

Smythe continued to study the toes of his shoes, not looking up to risk eye contact with any of us on the panel. Dixon continued.

"Reverend Gordon often interrupts the scheduled programming to give impromptu sermons when the mood strikes him. He often records his messages to the faithful from home or where ever else he might be, but they are always supposed to be coming directly from the church. He says it's much more credible if it looks like it comes from the source, gives the faithful the idea that he is always there for them and he never sleeps.

"During Hurricane Ike, Reverend Gordon really boosted his image with his flock by constant broadcasts from his hurricane home purported to be from the church in Corpus where winds were blowing over a hundred miles an hour and rain was driving sideways into the town. Everyone wanted to believe that their fearless pastor had remained in the church in spite of the storm, begging God to spare their house of worship. It was a favorite joke among church elders who were in on the ruse."

CHAPTER TWENTY SIX

When we took a break I called Yolanda to make sure she was okay. She told me was planning to drive to Beccah's safe house soon. She was getting spooked hanging around the office. "I'm taking my laptop and my phone," she said. "Let me know when you're heading back and I'll join you at the office. I love you, Dave Holman!" I told her I loved her too and would see her real soon.

Back in the conference room, we talked to other cops who were members of Gordon's church. These officers were able to give us more information about the church's property holdings. A senior member of the traffic division informed us that most of the properties owned by the church were held in Gordon's sister's name. Elizabeth Anne Gordon was the name we should be looking for to locate property deeds.

After that, we quickly found the hurricane house in Cuero. Actually, it was a few miles outside Cuero in DeWitt County. Millar immediately called the Cuero Police and asked that either they or the DeWitt County Sheriffs raid the premises and report back to him.

With the information from Dixon that there was a church retreat in the Rio Grande Valley and using Elizabeth Anne's name we were also able to locate acreage owned by the church just outside Harlingen. Calls to the Cameron County Sheriff's office got cooperation from that agency.

Saldana also posted more officers at the church campus and the compound on Mustang Island to observe in case Gordon should come back to either place. He chose to send mostly black and Hispanic officers who had no affiliation with the Church of the Eternally Blinding Light.

"Sergeant Mendoza, who I earlier posted to the church, is a devout Catholic and no fan of the Reverends," Saldana told me. "Another of my early choices was Officer Gene Mobley, who is black. Mobley told me that when he first came to Corpus and joined the force, he heard that many of his fellow policemen attended the Church of the Eternally Blinding Light. Mobley decided to try the place, seeking a spiritual home. The man later relayed to me that when he had taken a seat in the large church hall, other parishioners moved their mostly white families from the pews around him, leaving him isolated. These people continued to stare at him until he had gotten tired of their obvious intolerance, stood up and left in the middle of the service.

"I have Mobley in charge of the island compound with two other of my Corpus men and a handful of Port Aransas officers. The God's Security people at both locations have been relieved of their weapons, for their own safety we told them."

John stuck his head into the room to tell us that the Cuero Police had dispatched a team to search the Reverend's so-called hurricane house. No word had come back and my stomach was rumbling. I needed a meal and a good stiff drink, so I told Saldana and Millar I was going home for the night. "I'll be back tomorrow at first light," I told them.

CHAPTER TWENTY SEVEN

I called Yolanda and offered to swing by Beccah's place and escort her home. She was happy to take me up on the offer. When she came out of the house and got in the car, I suggested that we hit Rusty's for drinks. "No, Dave," my girl told me. "I think we need to kick back and relax at home. We've had enough for one day. I don't want to see any other people, I just want to snuggle up close to you and have you hold me!"

Back at our place, I fixed us martinis while Yolanda fried some shrimp and rice in coconut oil. With our meal, we switched to gin and tonics. I fetched the miniature TV from the office and we put on the news. The talking heads were showing photos of Gordon and pleading that anyone who saw the Reverend should call the Corpus Christi tip line. Other than the pleas for help there was nothing new in the search for Gordon, so we went to bed.

We were up at first light, quickly showered, dressed and headed out. I dropped my lady back at Beccah's and then aimed my Saab toward the city by the bay.

At the police building, another young uniform walked me to the elevator and rode up to the second floor with me. I found Millar and two other men I didn't know in the conference room pouring over piles of paperwork. "Saldana was here pretty late last night," Millar told me. "I told him to sleep in this morning so he'd be facing the day refreshed and with a clear head."

"Any news?" I asked.

"Apparently yesterday afternoon the De Witt County boys decided they wanted to be in on the raid of Gordon's house as it was on their turf, but it took them a few hours to get themselves ready and to liaise with the city cops. They got to the property just before dusk. The gate from the road, as well as the house itself, sported sophisticated high security locks that required special square-cut keys. They used cutters to snap the bolt on the gate and enter the property. Apparently they didn't find anyone outside on the land and no one answered their knock on the front or rear doors. The team debated for a while about whether or not they had enough cause to kick the door in or break a window."

"Geez, Louise," I sputtered, "country hicks! What did they need, some shots fired or a dead body?"

Millar gave me a look, then continued. "Finally, the Cuero chief told them to go ahead and break in, but they found the house empty. From the look of it, no one had been there for a month or more. The lawn was overgrown and the interior sported a thick layer of dust. They *did* find a sort of broadcast studio made to look like the altar of the real Church of the Eternally Blinding Light, but they reported that it looked like no one had been in that room in an even longer time."

"Another dead end," I said, just to be saying something, "anything else?"

"A clerk in the Cameron County tax office put in some overtime for us. She found two properties in Elizabeth Anne Jenkins name. One was a pricey condo on South Padre Island, the other was an eight acre spread near the old Air Force Base."

Millar smiled a cold smile and continued, "Cameron County

Sheriff Deputies went to the condominium tower out on the island. No one answered their knock, so they called for a warrant, got it emailed to them and entered the place. They found a recently slept-in unmade bed with dirty sheets and a closet full of sex aids, but no Reverend. They decided to bring the sheets back as evidence so we might learn if it was Gordon who had sex there and how recently."

"Could it be the Senator's little playpen?" I asked.

"Seems doubtful to me," Millar replied rubbing his hand over his face. "Anyway, a Harlingen SWAT team raided the Jenkins owned acreage, which had signage proclaiming it to be the Church of the Eternally Blinding Light Spiritual Retreat and seven-foot hurricane fencing festooned with 'no trespassing' and 'keep out' placards. They were admitted to the property by a party of church members who were staying there for some workshops. A couple church of brass hats were on the scene to conduct the classes, but no one would admit to having seen Reverend Gordon at the place."

"Oh, and Gordon did have a broadcast studio there arranged to look like the Corpus church," added one of the other officers with Ken Millar. "Actually, there was a whole complex of studios at that retreat. It looked like it was fixed up so they could send out feeds from the classrooms or the choir loft on the property just like they did from the main church."

"But no sign that Gordon had been there to record his message..."

"It would be a long shot anyway, Holman," Millar told me. "He'd have had to have flown that disc to Corpus, and besides, I don't think Kiii TV has that clear a signal all the way down in the valley."

"Don't they get Corpus stations on cable down there?" I inquired.

"Like I said, Holman, a long shot, we have better leads to follow..."

"Tell him about all these sightings," the other cop said with a lopsided grin.

"Gordon has been sighted?" I shook my head to clear any cobwebs. "Sighted, like something more than a few crank calls?"

Now both the other officers flanking Millar's chair started laughing. "Crank calls?" the other officer smirked and his partner laughed harder until Millar said, "Enough!"

"So what's this about sightings?"

"Oh," cop number two said, "we had hundreds of calls from people who said they'd seen Reverend Gordon all the way from North Beach to one of the water slides at *Schlitterbahn*. He was supposedly shopping at the HEB in Flour Bluff, fishing from the Fulton pier, arguing with a barista at the Starbucks on Staples that she's served him tepid coffee, taking a test drive in a new Alpha Romeo at the Fiat Studio on SPID..."

"The man was everywhere at once," chuckled cop number one.

"Yeah," put in a serious faced Ken Millar. "And then we discovered that the church's cable TV network was running a message to their viewers every fifteen minutes, telling them to put an end to Christian harassment in the area by calling the police tip line with false sightings of their beloved and innocent pastor. What a waste of our time!"

"I can't believe how twisted this guy is," Saldana said, entering the room with a white bakery box under his arm. "There isn't anything straight forward about him.

"I just heard from Mobley that they had a situation a few minutes ago. One of the God's Security men had brought out a hidden gun from somewhere and threatened to shoot any officer who came near enough to him. The man then led them on a wild chase through the out buildings and garden sheds near the front of the property. When they managed to get him cornered, he threw down the weapon, which turned out to be a realistic child's toy; the man laughed and said he just wanted to see how fast they could run!"

Mobley also reported that they'd heard a helicopter flying over the Gulf while the man had their full attention. "One of my men thought he heard it land briefly," he told them. "The bird was white. Beyond that it was difficult to see against the sun boiling out of the Gulf waters. We had assumed it was a Coast Guard patrol."

"We checked with the Coast Guard," Millar said. "There were no Coast Guard helicopters in the air this morning. We're assuming now that Gordon must have had a secret hidey hole somewhere on the property. His gunman was very likely running interference while others snuck him out to the beach and possibly onto a waiting helicopter. That would lead us to suspect that the Reverend had been hiding somewhere on the property since he recorded his little video speech. But if that was the case, he is gone now. We have to consider that he may have flown out on that chopper after recording his message."

Later in the morning, Mobley called again. A careful search

of the property around the big house had turned up a back stair-way behind the house where there had been a compost heap the night before. "My men descended those steps to find a large base-ment. One corner of the place was a second sound studio, decorat-ed just like the one we previously found upstairs, to look just like the church altar. It was accompanied by a small sound booth in the other corner at that end of the cellar."

From there, the morning was filled with speculation about where Gordon could be. Had he been at his home all along? Had he flown away in a conspiracy orchestrated by his security people? And if he had flown away, where did he go? Did the man own a yacht that was stationed somewhere out in the Gulf?

We began a search of Texas marine vessel registrations, under Gordon's name, his sister's name and even under Elizabeth Anne Gordon, just in case he might have such a vessel to which he could escape. By mid day nothing had been found. It looked like the case was slipping away from us. We got a call from the Feebs asking if we knew anything new, although they were unwilling to share any hunches they had.

Around two-thirty we received a report that a Nueces County Sheriff's team had raided the headquarters of God's Security Com-pany which was out Highway 44 halfway to Robstown. Apparent-ly, an off-duty deputy who was also a follower of Gordon's had tipped the security company's staff about the impending visit. The sheriff's team arrived to find filing cabinets dumped on the floor. Out in back of the office, guards in their security uniforms were feeding files and other documents into the flames that rose from the cut half of a fifty-five gallon drum that had been turned into a barbeque. The man who delivered the report told us that one of the arrested security operatives had told him that the cops had no idea of the size and scope of what they were messing with. "We have a small army of God's followers," the man had told him, "and we will be victorious!"

Saldana and Millar both shook their heads at this sad event. "These church folks seem intent on turning Gordon into some kind of persecuted martyr," Saldana said with downcast eyes. "I just don't know how we can deal with so many people who think this racketeer is the messiah!"

CHAPTER TWENTY EIGHT

J ust after four, a tall, uniformed Texas Ranger came to the door of our little operation center. "Lieutenant Saldana?" he asked sending his eyes around the room.

"I'm Saldana, what have you got for me?"

"Not great news, I'm afraid," the ranger told him. "One of our intelligence people up in Austin uncovered a connection between Gordon's security force and one of those renegade border-guarding militia groups. They've got some kind of serious encampment out beyond Alice. From what we've been able to uncover, they have over a hundred members, mostly out-of-work redneck trouble makers, many of them bikers and ex-cons. According to one source, they also have a large cache of weapons; assault rifles, grenade launchers, even a couple helicopters."

Millar lowered his head with a defeated look. "How are we supposed to deal with this? It sounds like Gordon has declared war on us!"

"He already told us that in the video," I reminded Millar.

"Video?" the ranger took off his cowboy hat, came in, took a seat and introduced himself as Sam Crockett. "Tell me about this video."

The media cart was still in the corner of the room, so the young office named John fired the equipment up and we played the message for the Texas Ranger. Ranger Crockett stared intently at the small screen until the message ended.

"I think war is the right word for it," he said when the screen went blank. "This Gordon is a very dangerous mega maniac!

"And that's part of why I came here. I wanted to see that we're on the same page in this investigation. I've got two battalions of Texas National Guardsmen heading toward Alice, where they're going to meet up with more state troopers and Jim Wells County deputies."

"Do you think Gordon could be there with these goons?" I asked.

"Difficult to say. I've got a couple state troopers in the area keeping the place under surveillance, but no one has spotted Gordon yet, which is not to say he isn't there. Also, there's only one helicopter present. Gordon could be with the other bird, wherever it is."

"So what's the plan, Crockett? How soon do you intend to enter the property?" Saldana asked. "I'd like to come with you, if that would be alright. I would really like to be in on Gordon's capture if possible."

"The colonel with the senior guard unit thinks we should continue to observe for awhile to get a better idea what we're up against," Crockett told us. "He's recommending we move in just before dawn."

I stood and told the assembled officers that they wouldn't need me for a military operation. "I should probably get some rest and report back here in the morning. Hopefully by then, you'll either have Gordon in custody or he'll be dead. Right now I need some time to myself."

"Yeah, you could use a break, Holman," Millar nodded. "Thanks for coming in and helping."

"Maybe if I take one of my meditative walks on Rockport Beach, I can put two and two together and arrive at six." I told them. I felt like I just wasn't carrying my load sitting in their conference room listening to more bad news. The thought that Gordon was close by while orchestrating his taunting of all the law enforcement involved just kept eating away at me.

"I'll let you know if I have any real brainstorms," I told them.

I drove a few short blocks to the Seafood Station Brewery, where I ordered a pint of the Rye IPA and sat thinking. If I was Gordon, what would I do? Well, that didn't work because, obviously, Gordon was madder than the March Hare and I was only a little crazy. I knew I'd lived most my life out where the busses don't run, as they say, but Gordon, he seemed to live, or at least *think* he lived, on some blessed heavenly cloud above all us foolish mortals. He suffered a plain and simple God complex!

And what would God do if he was suddenly called out for being the Oz man behind the screen, I asked myself.

I ordered a second pint, but it wasn't helping to clear my head. I needed that beach walk... but then I remembered that Yolanda always said I couldn't really meditate worth a shit after I started drinking. I downed my second pint and decided I didn't have much choice. I had to find an answer, and fast.

Gordon might have a small army ready to attack at any time, or at least a somewhat trained and coordinated mass of zealots prepared to defend their self-appointed god of a leader at all costs. I had to get out on the beach and try my best. Tell my psyche that I was up against a wall and I just had to get some cosmic answers!

I paid my tab and went out to my Saab. The motor kicked over on the first try, which I saw as a good sign, since it was a thousand miles overdue for an oil change and the heat had recently been brutal.

I tried to concentrate all the way home, through Portland, Gregory and Aransas Pass. With each town I passed, I wondered if Gordon could somehow be hiding there. He had faithful followers all up and down the coastal bend, in addition to a small army and a skilled security company.

I knew something was amiss as I turned off 35 onto Market Street. From the highway off-ramp I could see a white helicopter with an eye and a scarlet cross painted on the door hovering near the feed store where I had my office. I raced ahead, passing a couple pickup trucks on the left facing on-coming traffic, one sporting a large confederate flag from the bed. I pulled into my lot just as the chopper was touching down. I tried to ram the whirlybird, but a God's Security van blocked my path and spilled out a trio of big shouldered men in black outfits and ski masks. One of the masked men drew an ugly little automatic and fired a burst of shells into the radiator of the Saab, releasing a cloud of steam. Two other hooded men were coming down my stairs. They had Yolanda between them. Her hands and elbows were tightly bound behind her with silver duct tape and another strip of tape covered the bottom of her face. She tried to trip her captors, kicking at their feet, but they just lifted her higher as they rushed toward the waiting helicopter.

Why hadn't she stayed in hiding at Beccah's, I asked myself.

What was she doing at the office?

Yolanda put up a hell of a fight for a tied woman. She managed to swing her knees into the crotch of one of her kidnappers, who fell away to the side, but another man came forward, swung both hands in a vicious blow to Yolanda's face, then grabbed her around her waist and helped toss her onto the deck of the revving helicopter. The other men piled back into their van and headed for Highway 35.

The helicopter rose above the trees and dipped towards the coast. I tried to start the Saab, but it just sputtered and died. I ran around behind the feed store building and found Yolanda's old VW Thing. The keys were under the mat, where she often left them. The old four-banger caught on the second try. I ran back to the Saab and retrieved the battery powered blue flasher I kept in the glove box for emergencies. It might just come in handy. I also retrieved an old Los Angeles County sheriff's badge I had stolen some years before and pinned the star into my billfold, then I popped the clutch and aimed the old motor toward the coast road, where I could keep an eye on where the bird might be taking my girl.

The pursuit was almost too easy. The helo clung close to the shore on its southbound flight. I figured they would probably be heading for Reverend Gordon's compound on Mustang Island. I didn't actually think it through any farther than that. I got the old German crate up to its top speed, somewhere just over eighty, as I flew down the mostly empty two lane. The few vehicles I encountered I simply flew around without a problem.

Then I was entering Aransas Pass, where the limit was 35 mile per hour, I lit up my blue flasher and placed it on the dash as the car was topless and there was no roof to set it on. I got through the town with only a couple close calls. No Aransas Pass cops, thank God!

The chopper veered east, as I suspected it would, and I got my first wake-up call when I saw the light up sign on Highway 361. They were advising a two-hour wait for the ferry boat to Port Aransas and Mustang Island. If I had to wait in the queue for a ferry, Yolanda would be lost! I just had to press on ahead and bluff my way through the best I could.

I saw the end of the line stopped just short of the dock for the Aransas Casino gambling boat. Brake lights stretched forward toward the Intercoastal waterway and exhaust fumes rose in the air. Then there was a sign, "Park and Ride Customers Use Shoulder." With my blue light flashing, and without slowing from the old bomb's top end, I began my suicidal race down the outside edge of the highway. I nearly clipped a few folks who were hanging out onto the verge, and almost rear-ended a big twin cab turning right into a fishing camp, but I made it up to the ferry landing in just under seven minutes!

At the ferry landing, I skidded around the workers directing traffic, cut off the closest line and bounced onto a nearly loaded ferry just before they put up the gate to leave the dock. The rear of my Thing was scraping against the steal gate when it raised at the back of the deck. I was instantly surrounded by security people, one of whom had a gun out and aimed at me.

I put my hands up, smiled and said, "Special agent David Holman. I'm on a case. Can you let me get some ID out please?

The gun lowered, but wasn't re-holstered. I eased my wallet out of my pants and quickly flashed my bogus sheriff's badge, but it was enough. I tipped my head skyward, toward the white helicopter just ahead of us.

"Someone stole one of Reverend Gordon's helicopters," I improvised. "They've got a hostage on board. I've got to keep up with them as best I can. I can't lose them before the Texas Rangers can get on the trail. They should be coming up from Corpus to meet me. If I can just keep that bird in sight…"

It took a few seconds, but one of the ferry security guys, a thin blonde man wearing corporal's stripes, smiled and the others followed suit.

"Sure," he said. "Anything we can do to help?"

"I've already radioed ahead," I lied. "If you could just clear this lane first so I don't lose precious time."

"We can do that," the corporal told me nodding his head.

True to his word, the man quickly waved ahead the cars in front of me and I was off the ferry, but as I reached the dock, a pair of Port Aransas Police SUVs were waiting on either side of the exit lane. They pulled forward, nose to nose and blocked my path.

A large Port A cop grabbed me around my shoulders and pulled me over the door of the Thing slamming me face down onto the ferry landing asphalt. I recognized his partner as one of the Reverend's goons who had been present in the old barn the first time Gordon had beat me up. Then they were reading me my rights and arresting me, something about assault and impersonating a police officer, more plastic cuffs and I was shoved into the back of one of the police cars, the smiling officer making sure he cracked my skull against the roof of the vehicle and laughing.

The driver of the cop car raced right past the Avenue A turning for the Port Aransas jail and continued down Highway 361 out of town. We raced past the road to Island Moorings Marina and the golf course, flying down the highway at top speed with sirens roaring. We passed the entrances to the Beachwalk neighborhoods and Cinnamon Shores, finally turning toward the beach by a long high wall; Clem Gordon's compound. We were waved through both gates and came to a stop at a Cape Cod style four story building smack in the center of the enclosed area. I noticed that there were more men in God's Security uniforms. Three of them armed with assault rifles were guarding a group of Corpus Christi and Port Aransas police officers who sat on the ground up against the big house hands cuffed behind them. The whirlybird I'd been chasing was on the ground along with another identical aircraft. Both were white and painted with the security people's eye superimposed over a scarlet cross, only this logo stated that these birds belonged to God's Army.

My uniformed handlers dragged me from their vehicle, dropped me on the asphalt parking area where other men in white grabbed my ankles and pulled me across the pavement toward the massive structure.

CHAPTER TWENTY NINE

The Reverend's security men roughly tossed me down a flight of stairs at the back of the house and I landed on a stone floor, still in those infernal plastic cuffs. Looking around, I clocked that the north end of this damp hellhole looked just like the altar of Gordon's main church. They must have tossed me where they'd shot Gordon's video! Could this be a coincidence? At the other end of the cellar sat my lady. Yolanda was tied to a heavy high back chair with arms on it. Her ankles were tied to the chair legs, her knees spread wide and fastened to the armrest supports, and her arms to those armrests.

I tried to scoot myself closer to Yolanda's chair, to see if she was okay. Her face appeared swollen and she had a mix of blood and drool in one corner of her mouth.

"You wouldn't be trying to look up my dress, would you, Holman. You're a horny old bastard!"

"Hey, thank you too! I was trying to rescue you. I chased their helicopter all the way to Port Aransas to try and save you!"

"You and your white knight syndrome! You can't save the entire world, Holman. You're good, but you're not that good!"

"Yo, I really need to confess, I'm not really such a good guy at all. White knight syndrome? I don't know about that. I knew I had to try and rescue you, babe. You mean a lot to me!

"I have my prejudices... And my imperfections. I talk a good line about respecting everyone and their beliefs, but..."

Yolanda laughed, but then lifted her head back hard against the chair, pain written on her dark, pretty face. Something had to be really wrong that the simple act of laughing would hurt like that!

"Put a sock in it, Holman," she said as the pain passed. "I know you're not perfect! Nobody is! We all have our dark little secrets. Before we die here maybe I should share some of mine. Like the fact that a lot of my 'spirituality' is a big hoax, if you haven't figured that out already."

"But it's your Indian nature to be spiritual, isn't it? Like Gandhi and Krishnamurti."

Yolanda laughed again. This time it appeared to be even more painful. She took a couple deep breathes and let her shoulders sag.

"I mean you come from New Delhi…"

Yolanda gave that a smaller, less pained laugh. "More like new delicatessen! You assumed too much, Holman. You bought into my act so fast when you met me working in the Indian Palace…. I didn't want to disappoint you. I'm really just a Brooklyn girl."

I gave her a questioning look. "The sing-song speech? You pull that off pretty well when you want to."

"Well, my father *is* half Indian. My mother was one-hundred-percent Russian Jew. They inherited my grandfather's deli and decided they would include some Middle-Eastern and Asian dishes on the menu as the community was becoming more diverse. Things aren't always what they seem…

"But all this is just craziness. Not something to worry about right now. We need to be thinking of some way to get out of here. We need to let the Senator know that Gordon killed his sister. We've got to bring Gordon down and that entire phony church scam with him!

"But I'm feelin' a bit weak right now, Dave, so you'll have to do the major part of the thinking for us." With that, her head lolled sideways and her eyes closed.

"Yo?"

"I'm still here," she mumbled softly, "I'm just very tired."

I started looking around the room for something sharp I might rub my wrists against to cut the plastic ties. There was a rusting shovel in one corner. If I could sit on the handle to hold it stable while I ran the plastic along the blade…

Then I heard some shouting from somewhere, the house? Or the paved area behind it? There was gunfire and then there were running feet on the floor above me and the door to our prison flew open.

Bad news! It was Gordon, all red faced and angry. He had some kind of old wild-west gun, a long barrel six shooter dangling by his side. He came to stand over me and gave me a vicious kick in the ribs, then another aimed at my head. I managed to twist myself sideways so his foot missed me. Gordon lost his balance and fell on top of me, using some language that would definitely be out of place in church. He scrambled to get off me and gain his footing, but his considerable bulk was working against him.

"Damn you, Holman! You and your nigger bitch! You have cost me dearly! I want to kill you both, but I want you both to die slowly!"

"See you in hell," I managed, though most of the wind had

been knocked from my lungs.

The corpulent preacher finally got to his feet. He stood over me breathing hard, too spent to do anything for a minute or two. Then he remembered the six-gun in his hand. He raised it to aim at Yolanda's chest. I once again became aware of the hard footfalls in the house above. They seemed to be heading for the back door and the secret back stairs just off the porch that I'd been tossed down what seemed like hours ago.

And then Senator Jenkins was standing in the doorway, his face red and full of hate and a large and ugly automatic clenched in the white knuckles of both hands. He screamed and squeezed the trigger, firing over and over again. When his first bullet ripped into Gordon, the preacher's gun went off as well, but it was aimed high and simply sent plaster dust raining down from the ceiling. The Senator kept shooting until the slide stayed back and his gun was empty. While he fired, Clem Gordon's body performed a spastic dance against the wall behind me, his right arm waving his old west weapon up and down. After the last bullet ripped into his body, Gordon's fat carcass slowly slid down the wall, still shuddering with heavy spasms and leaving a thick bloody trail.

"She was my wife and I loved her," the Senator screamed at the top of his lungs from the doorway. "God damn you, Gordon. I loved her. She's the only woman I *ever* really loved!" The he burst into tears and slid down the doorframe to crumple on the floor. Behind him a pair of state trooper appeared with weapons drawn. "Cut those two loose," the Senator whispered. Then he sat up and said a little louder, "Cut'm loose! The detective and the girl. Get them loose and call some medics down here to check them out."

"Ambulance is already on the way, Senator," one of the Texas cops assured him. "It'll take a few minutes. They're coming from the Corpus end of the island as this is county land."

The other state policeman walked over by me and gave a questioning look at the bloody hunk of Swiss cheese that had been Pastor Gordon after he cut my plastic wrist cuffs with a large hunting knife from his belt.

"He drew down on me," the Senator said without a smile. "I came down to rescue my friends here and he brought up his weapon to shoot me."

The trooper looked at me. I shrugged. "Must be like the Senator said, it all happened pretty fast and I had my eyes closed as the preacher was kicking me in the guts." I tried to rub some circulation back into my numb wrists.

The first policeman had cut Yolanda's binding, but she remained slumped in her chair, although she did manage a smile and a whispered "Thank you."

Normal color was returning to the Senator's face. He sat up straighter, composing himself. "Leave us alone here for a few minutes, would you?" he asked the two cops. When the troopers gave each other bewildered looks, he continued. "I ain't going to be tampering with any evidence. I just have a few confidential questions for my friend Holman here and the girl. They're private detectives and they are workin' for me, damn it! I need to verify some of the facts in all this."

One state policeman cocked his head to the side, the other shrugged his shoulders and they started up the stairs. Then one of them turned back towards us. "You've got a mess upstairs, Senator, and a bit of carnage outside. Looks like the preacher had a pretty good sized army fighting for Jesus." The other cop laughed.

When the troopers were up the stairwell and out of earshot, the Senator spoke. "He killed his *own* sister! My wife.... Gordon was a lowlife animal. He was pond scum.... He killed her to make sure I'd stay in office, just to protect his little empire!" The Senator was quiet for a few beats. His eyes were closed, though still leakin' tears.

"He was doin' her when I met her, doin' his *own* sister! Had been since he was twelve and she was seven.... Then she started goin' out with me. She said she came to me hopin' I could protect her. I did my best. She was already pregnant with his kid and after we got together, he kept her under his thumb, constantly remindin' her that the abortion I helped her to obtain was her ticket to hell, no salvation ever.

"She loved her brother and she believed him, she *believed* in him! Every God damn lie he told her! And I believe she loved me too.... Damn it all, she *did* love me!"

"It's okay, Senator," Yolanda whispered, quickly opening her eyes and surveying the room before she closed them again.

"Winning just ain't so damn important anymore, Holman," the Senator announced in a louder voice. "I sold my soul to the devil, now I need to try and buy it back if I can! I plan to spend my last days in office tryin' to do some good for the people of Texas. And if they choose not to re-elect me, that's just fine! I'll find something more useful to do with my time. Ma'm," he addressed in Yolanda's direction. "Maybe you can help me set up a charity. But one that can rescue people instead of elephants."

EPILOGUE

It was one of those monster media events. All the news networks had vans in the parking lot of the Church of the Eternally Blinding Light, and bristles of microphones sprouted from stands at the front of the hastily assembled stage. Senator Burt Jenkins sat center stage between an assortment of state and local dignitaries along with two of the church elders.

The Senator was dressed all in white, looking something like the Kentucky Fried Colonel in a ten-gallon hat and a bolo tie featuring a diamond encrusted cross. His face was fully exposed without his reflector sunglasses; his back was straight and his shoulders high and proud. At a signal from somewhere off stage, he stood and stepped up to the tree of mics.

"I am here today to let everyone know that I will not be seeking re-election to another term in this great state's legislature. After the events of the past few weeks, I feel that I have much work to do on my own life.

"The recent deaths of my wife and my brother-in-law, Pastor Clemson Gordon have brought me to some much needed introspection and given me new responsibilities in my life. Reverend Gordon was using the great power entrusted to him by the Lord in ways that were evil and self-serving. He and a handful of others in this church became corrupted by the power they held in their hands, and they used that power to hurt and enslave the very people who needed the Lord's help most. This in turn has caused me grief in addition to the sadness I carry in losing my loving wife of almost thirty years.

"I believe I am needed right here, to help rebuild our church and restore the world's confidence in this great institution. In recent meetings with our deacons and elders, we have decided that we will not seek a new head minister, but will instead share the responsibility of doing the Lord's work equally among all the faithful in this organization. Our Bible studies will be democratic meetings where all can share their interpretation of the scriptures rather than one or two people dictating the meaning there-in. Any church member in good standing may have the opportunity to preach a sermon to us, so we will have the views of all our parishioners and we may debate those views to help us reach a stronger truth.

"And finally, the doors of this house of worship will be open to *all* who wish to come in no matter what the color of their skin or what their sexual orientation. Jesus said "Love thy neighbor," and in this church we will welcome and love *all* our neighbors! We may lose some of our following who choose to disagree with this idea, but I believe we'll gather so many more to the fold by being honest, open and loving! I intend to use all the illegally gotten gains that this church donated to my re-election campaign to help feed poor children, to care for our veterans and senior citizens, to fight against prejudice of all kinds and to make the world a better place! This is a big job. It may be difficult for me at first, but I'll learn how. I'll do everything I can, I promise you all!"

The election was less than three weeks away. I was pretty sure the ballots had already been printed and the Senator's name would be on them, the only Republican name for the seat he had held. Then Yolanda gave voice to exactly what I'd been thinking, "I'll bet he wins the election anyway," she told me with a coy wink. "And, I'll bet he can't say no to it!"

www.ingramcontent.com/pod-product-compliance
Lightning Source LLC
Chambersburg PA
CBHW051922240626
47153CB00004B/1331